D0485797

Out of the corner of his eye, through his dark aviator glasses, he saw her jogging toward him but he didn't let on. Shorts, long legs, hiking boots, hair chopped off about half an inch from her head.

He went on doing what he was doing, which was jotting his time and location in his log. He could hear her panting as she jogged up.

"You're Forest Service."

"How'd you guess?"

"A bear's attacked somebody up in the meadow," she said. "I've come for help."

He tossed the clipboard and ballpoint back through the window.

"Bears in these parts don't attack nobody. This ain't Yellowstone," he said without looking at her.

"I'm no expert on bears. I'm telling you what I saw. Somebody's dead up there."

He let his eyes move slowly down her. See what she'd do with that. She didn't do anything but look straight back at him. He didn't care for that look.

By Cecil Dawkins
Published by Ivy Books:

THE SANTA FE REMBRANDT
CLAY DANCERS
RARE EARTH

Books published by The Ballantine Publishing Group
are available at quantity discounts on bulk purchases
for premium, educational, fund-raising, and special
sales use. For details, please call 1-800-733-3000.

RARE EARTH

Cecil Dawkins

IVY BOOKS • NEW YORK

Ivy Books
Published by Ballantine Books
Copyright © 1995 by Cecil Dawkins

Library of Congress Catalog Card Number: 95-94543

ISBN 0-8041-1262-2

Manufactured in the United States of America

First Edition: December 1995

10   9   8   7   6   5   4   3   2   1

Prologue

The stars descend the earth departs
the cold of heaven rimes our hearts
. . . .
reject you battered and despised
and ask salvation of the skies

What does he mean, writing this stuff? He's a country-western singer, isn't he? Well, these are not country-western lyrics. She might be just a kid but she knows that much.

He's scribbled them on the back of a pub shot of Ginger and Kylie. Both dead now, burned beyond recognition. Ginger identified by nothing but an earring. They said the other one was Kylie because Kylie was supposed to be pilot that day. Blamed the crash on fog coming in off the Mississippi, but it could have been fog coming off Kylie's brain.

Galen has scribbled the words in pencil so faint they're hard to read. Maybe it's just an old poem by Omgreeb. Omgreeb used to write poems for her, but they were more like nursery rhymes for a little kid such as she'd been when he spun out for her entertainment the Adventures of Omgreeb, King of the Arctic Animals. They went something like, If Lindsey takes time

1

to count her toes, she'll discover she has more toes than woes.

They were meant to cheer her up when the three of them—Ginger and Kylie and Galen—went on tour and left her behind in the Nashville mansion with her nurse Hattie. Galen would record on cassettes the episodes in the ongoing story of Omgreeb and stick them under her pillow like something from the tooth fairy. Omgreeb was an Eskimo prince, but the king and queen of the Eskimos set him out on an ice floe to die because he was a royal disgrace. He had gills instead of a nose and flippers instead of hands. And as he lived in a very cold place, he grew an extremely thick skin made of scales the hues of the rainbow, which ingeniously drew warmth from the thin Arctic sun.

In the pub shot, Ginger wore a sun grin and Kylie wore a hat.

M'lindy is lying belly-up on the foot of the bed, holding her head in her arms to shut out the light. Lindsey drops the photograph on the king-size bed and buries her face in M'lindy's fur. M'lindy squirms out of her arms and shoots to the top of the drapes.

Lindsey has locked herself in the master bedroom, which is the tour bus's rear compartment. It's Galen's now, but he said she could have it while he's away. And she doesn't intend to come out till Galen comes down off that mountain. When she told him so, he just laughed at her. "You're a weird little kid, you know it, Lindsey?"

"Come on, babycakes, open up."

Byron, on the other side of the door. At it again.

"The ice cream's melting, honey."

Who said I wanted any?

"Come on. Open up. This ice-cream cone's dripping down my arm."

Chill out, Byron. Get a life.

What a creep. Twenty-seven years old if he's a day, and her going on eleven.

"Look, you got me for eight thousand three hundred and some-odd dollars. You said you'd give me a chance to win some of that money back."

I never said any such thing.

She'll never see a cent of that money anyway. It's all on paper. And gin rummy is not what he's after. Lindsey knows that.

"I'm eating mine. It's pistachio. You know how you love pistachio."

She does. She loves pistachio. You can taste the green.

"You don't open that door, I'll eat yours, too."

You do that, Byron.

It's only Thursday afternoon. The tour bus arrived late yesterday at the Taos rodeo grounds, and Galen inspected the lights and met with the technician and gave him the color gels and arranged for a man to help with the setup. Then he left at dawn this morning while the bus was still sleeping. And if she knows him he won't be back till just before Saturday's concert. And meanwhile left her here with this creep outside the door.

Parting the wraparound drapes, she peers out the wraparound rear window. Nothing out there but the rodeo grounds where they'll hold the concert Saturday night, and a big cottonwood tree with a couple of Indian men squatting on their heels in the shade.

M'lindy lets herself backwards halfway down the drapes and jumps. She stretches out on the bottom of the bed and glares at Lindsey out of electric blue eyes. M'lindy is bored witless because she can't go outside.

"That makes two of us," Lindsey tells her. She has laid in a supply of potato chips and Milky Ways and a can of mixed nuts and some nectarines, but she's not sure they will last her. When are you coming down off that mountain, Galen? When will you draw a comb through your golden hair and recall that you are the best singer and steel player the world has ever known? When will you stop scribbling stuff nobody can understand and write some more heartwarming lyrics people can relate to because they are the very stories of their lives?

Byron whispers through the door, "Come on, baby-cakes, I want to keep you company."

Like I care.

She turns on the TV and flips the remote to TNN. Somebody she doesn't know is singing what might be an old Waylon Jennings song about being a stranger in a world he doesn't know. All she has to do is look out the window at the New Mexico landscape to identify with that.

1

Gin knows she's on Indian land and if she gets caught she'll be in trouble. But she pulls off and parks the rig behind a cluster of piñon and juniper. It's Friday morning. She has a three-day weekend ahead of her. She locks up and shoulders her backpack.

Then all she has to do is part limp strands of barbed wire and step through, cross ten acres of rolling pasture, and she's home free, safe in the piñon belt at the foot of the mountain. She's not afraid of being caught because tomorrow, Saturday, is San Geronimo, the pueblo saint's name day, and the people would be busy getting ready for the footrace and the arrival of traders from pueblos downriver. She'll have the trail to herself.

She knows better than to backpack in the mountains alone. The rule of thumb is, you go with a couple of friends. Then if somebody gets hurt, one of you stays with the injured party while the other goes for help. But she wants the mountains to herself, with nothing to chatter at her but the birds, and higher up maybe a marmot whistling from a safe distance on top of a rock. With luck maybe she'll startle a deer. Probably not. It's close to hunting season, when they're smart enough to retreat to the farthest ends of the wilderness.

The easy thing would have been to drive up to the ski valley like most backpackers, and leave the rig, short for rigor mortis, which is what they have called the ancient station wagon since the time it sat moribund for months, till the whole compound—Tina and Reuben and Croy and Gin, and even their sweet, spacey landlady Magda Sanchez—chipped in for new tires and battery. But she chooses to steal across pueblo land for a solitary shortcut to the austere beauty of the rim. For she's got a problem, and she likes to take her problems to the mountain.

First, she noticed something different with Reuben, something tentative, unsure, a little shy, which was definitely unlike him. She saw it as soon as he and Tina came home from the summer dig and wondered what it was. Then she saw him looking at Tina, who was just sitting on the floor talking—with her hands, as usual. Oh, no! He was smitten with Tina and feeling foolish about it.

She'd felt it like a punch in the solar plexus, like betrayal. Why? Afraid this could break up the group? Feeling excluded? Jealous? She told herself jealousy is definitely a low vibration, but natural. You can lose your best friend to a lover, though that had never happened before. They'd always joked about Tina's lovers, discussed them, taken them apart. How was Reuben different? He just was, that's all.

She's told herself he'll get over it, Tina's not his type. His type is blond and buxom, and Tina is small and dark. She's watched them together. She's sure that Tina, who knows everything, doesn't know this.

The Indian trail soon brings her to where a pinch in the canyon takes her into the stream itself with her boots tied together and slung around her neck. Hiking barefoot through ice water in September is not her recreation of choice, but soon enough she's winding upward through ponderosa pine and Douglas fir. The trail brings her ever closer to the sun.

Her backpack weighs thirty-six pounds. Forget one little thing, you can find yourself high and dry on top of a mountain. So she keeps a list she consults as she packs: socks, underwear, long johns for sleeping, toothbrush, toothpaste, soap, towel, washcloth, trail mix, oatmeal mixed with powdered milk—she adds water and heats it for breakfast—jerky and dried fruit for lunch, several freeze-dried dinners . . .

Tucked into crannies: kitchen matches in film canisters to keep them dry, folds of toilet paper, a headband, and a slouch hat for the heat of the day on the ridge. And rolled on top of the pack, behind her shoulders, a Thermarest mattress, a combination rain poncho/drop cloth, and her down sleeping bag.

She carries her Swiss Army knife in her pocket, and, suspended from her belt, binoculars, water bottles, four-ounce flashlight, sheathed hunting knife, stainless steel all-purpose eating/drinking cup, and a flask of tequila, Jose Quervo Gold.

In late morning she hits the aspen belt. At this altitude there's not much between you and the sun. She's wearing her Ray • Bans, but she stops in the shade to put zinc oxide on her nose. Overhead in the aspen leaves, birds she can't see are excited about something, maybe about her.

Then the trail surges upward in earnest. She can feel her lungs expand. The ground under her hiking boots is dappled with sun and shade. A chipmunk skitters across in front of her on urgent business, tail in exclamation mode.

A little farther and the sun is straight up. She decides to swap her jeans and sweatshirt for her many-pocketed hiking shorts and the clean T-shirt that, half asleep, she fished out of her drawer. A gift from her dyke friend Teakwood, it once was black with a motto in cerise that says Love Happens.

"Cheez, lookit what she's doing!" The kid nudges Ben Lopez in the ribs and gets ignored for his trouble.

While they watch, she stretches out those long legs and pulls off her pants. She digs in her backpack and brings out something khaki colored. Shorts. She's pulling on a pair of khaki shorts. Then off comes her sweatshirt. No bra.

"Lordy-lordy!" the kid exclaims.

Something about her intrigues Ben Lopez. Like maybe with that hair and skin she is not one hundred percent Anglo. At this distance he can't see her eyes.

He's a little disappointed when she ties the sweatshirt by its arms around her waist, shrugs into her pack, and crosses the stream, leaving tribal land. Down below, at the foot of the trail, they'd be going over whatever vehicle she's abandoned in the piñons and juniper, checking license plates through a state trooper who is one of their own. Ben Lopez doubts she's anything more than a backpacker, but they have to be sure.

The kid whispers, "We ought to follow her."

Ben watches her make her way up the trail. He's never seen her before, but he doubts she poses any threat. "You talk too much, Beaver."

The kid thinks they call him that because it's some kind of an Indian thing, but it's a joke. They call him that because he's so fidgety and talks all the time. "You got to learn the quiet way," Ben tells him.

"What's that, the quiet way? Some kind of a ritual or something?"

"You been reading too many books. If it was that kind of a 'way' it'd be Navajo, not Pueblo."

The boy fidgets beside him. Ben's father, the pueblo governor, has handed the kid over to him, giving him no choice in the matter. The kid's father, Arnold Martinez, Ben's mother's brother, who should have been a big man in Ben's life, ran away from the pueblo when he was young, claiming he wanted something better out of life than a mud village. For Ben's money, nothing could be better than several hundred thousand acres of prime mountain land for hunting, pure streams for fishing, and a close-knit community to belong to. Pueblos were the only Indians in the country who'd kept the land that they'd lived on for a thousand years.

"Even as a boy, Arnold was always chasing rainbows," Felipe, Ben's father, told him. "He was half the time up the mountain looking for a gold mine."

Arnold Martinez ended up going to L.A., making money shooting flaming arrows at covered wagons for the flicks, getting himself a bungalow in Beverly Hills, a fancy car with a top that went down, nearly drinking himself to death. Felipe went to L.A. and brought him back to the village. They dried him out, he married a Pueblo woman, they had a child, the boy kneeling beside Ben now. That lasted maybe a couple years. Then one day Arnold took the kid with him to town for some tenpenny nails, and that was the last they saw of either of them. He returned to L.A., played a Comanche chief, took an Anglo woman, and, for reasons Ben could only guess at, finished the job of drinking himself to death.

After Arnold Martinez died the kid went wild— joined a gang, played with drugs, then trouble with the law. The Anglo woman couldn't do anything with him. She talked Ben's father, the boy's maternal uncle, into helping the kid "claim his heritage," as she put it. It was that or a boot camp in Idaho.

When Ben met the Amtrak train in Lamy, the boy

swung down to the platform in Day-Glo shoes and a
pink punk haircut. Ben found a barbershop in Santa Fe
and had it all shaved off. The kid wept angry tears all
the way to Taos.

He acted like he was only at the pueblo because he
had to be. But he'd let his hair grow long and somewhere found himself a fringed shirt, and when the
money from his mother ran out and he needed shoes, he
was too proud to let them buy him a pair but made himself these weird-looking clubfooted moccasins out of
leather he'd picked up God knows where.

Sometimes the boy seems to be trying, but so igno-
rant he reminds Ben of the hippies out here in the six-
ties and seventies when Ben was a little kid. The
Indians laughed at them, living in their communes,
making a mess of farming, gawking at the dances, gorg-
ing themselves on the chili in the shrine meant only as
a symbolic offering to guests, calling themselves names
they thought sounded Indian—Canyon, Prairie Dog,
Willow—failing to notice that Pueblo Indians all have
Spanish names, ever since the Spanish missionaries
lined them up and baptized them, ready or not, centuries
ago. A pity, Ben thought, but nothing now to be done
about it.

Ben and the boy aren't alone on the northern border.
The others are strung out maybe fifty yards apart, keeping watch on the arroyo that marks the boundary of
tribal land. For days now, sent by the old men of the
council, they've come to the mountain before dawn.
They've all seen the girl, though she hasn't seen them.
The birdcalls relayed up the mountain attest to an alien
presence on Pueblo land. Usually they're not so particular about this northern border, but things have been
happening—strangers with surveying equipment wandering across from the ski valley or Forest Service land.

Alarmed, elders have called in the young men's society to keep this vigil. Outsiders are allowed up here only in the company of Pueblos.

The backpacker has a good body, lithe and lean, but female, definitely female. Though he'll be married next month, Ben can still appreciate that long stride. She knows what she's doing. She knows the way to make time up a mountain is not to hurry but to strike a slow, steady pace and keep it up. He rests his chin on his steepled fingers and watches her, what he can see of her through the trees, till she plows into a bend in the trail and disappears.

"You ought to've gone after her," the kid says.

"You want to go after her, go after her yourself."

The kid starts up, either taking him at his word or daring him. Ben grabs his shirttail and pulls him back down. "Hold your horses."

"I wisht I could."

The kid gets more Indian every day. Now it's horses.

Nearing the meadow below the ridge, Gin stops beside a log, shrugs out of her pack, and takes a water bottle off her belt, the new one with the cylinder inside. The night before you leave, you fill the cylinder and put the bottle in your freezer. Then next morning you fill the bottle before setting out and the frozen cylinder keeps it iced for hours. She knows she's a sucker for such inventions.

The wind's a sibilant whisper, bringing down aspen leaves like golden rain among the straight white stems of the forest. She puts together the sandwich makings she brought along in Ziploc bags—avocado and tomato slices, grated Monterey Jack, alfalfa sprouts—layering everything on pumpernickel. It's the last fresh meal she'll have till she comes out of the mountains. She takes her time eating it, then stretches out on the ground with her backpack for a pillow and dozes off. She's wakened by a sharp sound—aspen trunks, she thinks, knocked together by the wind. Lying there looking up through the aspen leaves is like looking at a sky full of yellow butterflies.

As she lies there contented, surrounded by beauty, she hears what sounds like a big dog growling. Probably an Indian dog—she's still not far from Pueblo land. She lies still, hoping it will go down the other side of the mountain. She has to be pretty close to the ridge. But the sound comes again, louder this time. A dog would need the lungs of a bull to put out that kind of roar. She sits up.

It comes again, a muted bark and then a low, ominous growl. She scrambles to her feet and looks toward the meadow. You don't have to fear bears in these mountains, do you? Not if you leave them alone. They are black bears and brown bears, not grizzlies.

But it might be a mother with a cub. Such matrons can be dangerous. Has it picked up her scent? A slow drum sets up under her ribs.

The roar comes again. From only a little way up the trail, probably in the meadow. It's definitely a bear and it's clearly annoyed.

She hoists her pack and trots back down the trail to wait till the growling subsides. But before she's gone very far she hears another sound, this one only too human. The cry comes again, weak, little more than a whimper. She brushes at an insect on her forehead, but it's the vein that awakes in times of stress and crawls from her hairline to the inner edge of her left eyebrow.

The low growl again, then the faint cry. She drops her pack and starts back up the trail. She's running, but at twelve thousand feet it feels more like slugging through heavy surf.

She bursts through the scrub oak fringing the meadow and halts. Twenty yards up the grassy slope a figure sinks slowly, one bloody arm shielding a mask of gore that has recently been a face, and over it a cinnamon bear towers on its hind legs, twisting its head slowly, heavily, one forepaw paddling the air. No cub in sight.

Growing up in the Sangre de Cristos you know what to do about bears. You make a racket. If that doesn't work, you hit him on top of the nose. She knows what you do about bears all right, but she's never been called on to do it.

The figure on the ground utters a strangled cry, like choking on its own blood. She surges forward, yelling, flailing like flagging down a train.

The massive head swings slowly around. The little eyes look at her. She stops. From the cavernous throat comes a tentative threat. The bear hesitates, seems to consider, and for a second looks like it might come down on all fours and lumber off in the brush. But instead it shifts its massive body and turns full around to face her, lifts its nose skyward, and opens its pointed muzzle. The roar that emerges shakes the mountain. She feels it in the soles of her feet. It echoes and re-echoes, and the echoes are followed by a large silence as if the mountain listens.

She thinks the figure on the ground has moved. Whoever he is, he's still alive. The bear stands there, weaving a little, watching her curiously, then tentatively turns back to the bloody victim.

What now?

Hit him on top of the nose.

But the bear is eight feet tall. You'd have to stand on

a chair to hit him on top of the nose. And hit him with what?

A limb bleached silver by the sun lies ten feet in front of her, as big around as a grandfather rattler. To get to it she'd have to move forward, and she can't make herself.

The bear swings side to side, heavily, as if undecided about something. One shaggy paw, as big around as a cow pat, fans at her like a warning: Go away. She makes herself meet those little eyes so out of proportion to that great body. The contact is intimate, terrifying. The figure on the ground moves again, reclaiming the bear's attention. She pounces on the broken branch.

With a startled grunt, the bear swings its massive head in her direction and roars loud enough to start an avalanche. Falling back she trips over a root. Faint with fear, her heart so big it crowds out the air, she scrambles up.

The bear hasn't moved. She circles in hopes of diverting its attention from the figure on the ground. It works. Now the bear is entirely focused on her. It turns clumsily, watching her, then in slow-motion comes down on all fours and moves toward her.

Ben and the Beaver have heard the bear. The kid shoots up again, ready to run—which way, to or from, Ben Lopez can only guess. He stops the boy by a firm grip on his shirttail and pulls him down. Birdcalls relayed down the mountain make it clear the bear is not on Pueblo land. Ben knows that already. But the girl could be in trouble.

"Stay here," he says to the kid, who looks like he wants to argue. With the cry of a rain crow, he relays the message up the mountain that he's going to investigate. He creeps up the hill, low to the ground, still on tribal land. The roar comes again and the girl puts up a racket yelling. Ben slips into the arroyo to cross the stream but is stopped by a voice behind him.

"The council forbids it."

It's Hank Sandoz, son of one of the powerful old men and in charge of the watchers on the mountain. Ben knows if he looks up the hill behind him he won't see anybody. He hesitates. The bear could be rabid, or a female with a cub.

Maybe the backpacker's scared it off, making such a racket. That showed good sense. He backs up the hill away from the stream, listening hard, but the mountain is quiet.

Gin watches with hypnotic fascination as the mouth slowly opens. The bear makes a silent, snapping feint, twisting its head aside like a dog trying to get rid of something caught in its teeth. The inside of its mouth is partly black as a Chow's, partly bubble-gum pink.

She tries summoning a prayer suitable to the occasion, comes up only with, Oh my God. Then for no discernible reason, with a series of grumbles and a disdainful glance in her direction, the bear swings aside and ambles off toward the woods, the big round powerful rump sashaying side-to-side as he goes, and so quick it's like magic, disappears in the low growth of oak and alder.

Weak from the plunge of adrenaline, trying to get her breath, she approaches the figure on the ground. Anglo, not Hispanic or Indian. The short face tapers from broad temples to a chin with a cleft. And the hair, what she can see of it matted with all that blood, is cut short on top and at the temples and flows down the back like a long blond mane. One leg is bent at an impossible angle, and through a tear in the bloody jeans, the unmistakable dead white of bone. A compound fracture, the arm so bent and bloody she can't find the hand. A massive head wound bleeds into the gravel. She drops to her knees, then to all fours, and gives up her avocado sandwich to the gravel of the scree. She spits out the bitter taste of bile and tries to get hold of herself.

She wets her *panhuello* from the water bottle on her belt and, battling fear and revulsion, bathes what's left of the face.

Is the victim alone?

She looks quickly around. The meadow is silent, empty. And no backpack, not even a fanny pack. A day hiker. Maybe an urban cowboy who lost his cool and did something to provoke the bear.

She pulls her thick, hooded sweatshirt from around her waist and folds it under the bloody head, takes her water bottle off her belt, and tips it to the crusted lips. "Drink!" she commands. She's heard somewhere that a voice of authority gives comfort even to the dying.

The eyelids flutter, the eyes roll, then slowly zero in and focus. The face goes into rapidly shifting configurations of shock and fear. There's no mistaking that whoever he is, he wants badly to escape her.

"You're safe," she tells him. "The bear's gone."

Calm settles on the bloody countenance. It must have been a striking face. She's seen it before but she can't think where. She takes the battered flask from her belt and tilts it to the torn lips. The tequila trickles down his chin and dilutes the blood. Fingers plow frantically into the bloody stomach, then grope for the zipper tab. Then up through the crusted lips comes a gush of blood that soaks her T-shirt. The eyes roll back in his head, taking with them all semblance of consciousness.

She knows even innocuous head wounds bleed copiously. Though she suspects her ministrations are hopeless, she tries to staunch the flow with her paisley *panhuello*. Can she leave him long enough to run down the trail for her pack?

No. There's still the bear.

In desperation she pulls the T-shirt over her head, wads it, and presses it to the head wound while she calculates. She's been climbing for about four hours. Even downhill all the way, it would take half that time to go back for help, and longer to return to the meadow, unless with horses.

The flow of blood from the lips lessens to a trickle. Rising to her knees she looks desperately around for help, knowing she won't find any. The meadow is beautiful and empty and still. When she looks back down at the figure in her arms, eyes startlingly blue look up at her.

"Who are you?" she asks. "What happened?"

The mouth works but the sound that emerges is unintelligible, like the imitation of a growl. "Grrrr."

"Yes," she says. "I saw the bear."

But now the fingers grasp her arm and she thinks he shakes his head.

"What? Tell me!"

But the eyes close. He has to be in shock, he has to be kept warm.

"Okay, look, I'm just going for my sleeping bag. It's not far. I'll be right back."

But the hand holds her fast. She removes it finger by finger from her arm and starts to rise. Then comes a gasp, and the next breath rattles. The blond head tries to lift, like trying to point with its pointed chin. She looks at the top of the cliff but has to shut her eyes against the glare.

A confusing mumble and she bends closer. "What?

What is it?" Her words sound crisp and definite, almost
angry. "Who are you? What's happened here?"

The trickle of blood from the parched mouth becomes
a foaming torrent, then stops. The white throat is covered with blood, and so is her own bare breast.

"Oh God," she breathes.

The bloody face falls toward her. To anyone watching
it might appear to be nuzzling her bare nipple, but she
knows what it's really doing is dying.

2

Lindsey puts a black four on a red five and moves up an ace. But all she turns up is another black four. M'lindy is underneath the drapes, looking out the window. Sol bores M'lindy to death.

The bus is getting stuffy. Why doesn't somebody turn on the air? She always wanted to travel in the old tour bus. Ginger and Kylie had quit using it. Got into flying instead. After the crash Lindsey made Galen promise never to fly without her permission, as he is all she has left in the world.

What once was Ginger and Kylie's king-size bed takes up most of the rear compartment, with cabinets, shelves to the ceiling, and built-in chests. TV and stereo set into the wall.

It's Friday. She tried to sleep late to make the time go faster, and for brunch had a Milky Way and a Coke sneaked from the refrigerator. No sign of anybody out front except Aunt Glad in her pink plastic eyeglasses with rhinestone corners, dressing up one of her dolls. "Come on out here, dearie," she calls. "Come look at Heidi."

Lindsey can do without Heidi. Heidi is the doll. She can do without Aunt Glad. Glad Hand. What a laugh. Glad is Kylie's widowed sister-in-law. She is also the mother of Byron and Griff. Byron is her favorite because Griff is, as she'll explain to just about anybody, "developmentally challenged." She explains this with a look that says it's just one more cross she bears.

Galen brought her along to look after Lindsey. Lindsey doesn't think she needs looking after. She works back through the deck one at a time. Some would call it cheating, but she couldn't care less. She doesn't have the patience to go through three-by-three. She gets a red queen for her black king, but that's all she wrote.

Where has everybody gone? She opens a package of potato chips. She is already sick of junk food. What makes Galen so hardheaded? He is something like the King of the Arctic Animals.

What would have happened if Omgreeb's ice floe hadn't bumped into that of the old woman set out on the cold dark sea to die, as is the Eskimo custom? The old woman turned out to be a wizard, and as Omgreeb comforted her in her final hours, with her last breath she bestowed on him fantastic powers and named him King of the Arctic Animals in the Pure Land of Ice and Snow.

Then along came a lost polar bear cub. Next the emperor penguin Anka, then the shabby but regal eagle, the lazy, good-natured sea lion, and the female whale Mumja, who couldn't fit on the increasingly crowded ice floe but who showed up in times of peril and leapt with surprising agility out of the Arctic ice to rescue Omgreeb.

The hike up the mountain is Galen's own private ceremony, his church-like. And left her down here with Aunt Glad and the band—Cory Lyn on the bass, and Jason Mason, the best steel she's ever heard except Galen. And of course Griff on the drums.

But he had to take Griff with him up the mountain. Why?

Because, he said, he needed him to help bring something down.

Galen is big but Griff is *real* big. Galen says he'd
make a first-rate NFL lineman if he could remember the
plays. She wishes he'd left Griff here. She could stand
a little company and Griff is a hoot, the things he'll say.
Like he'll go, "Jason he pushed in the bunk with Cory
Lyn and she knocked him out on the floor." If Griff
says it, it's the truth. He doesn't know how to lie. He
doesn't look at all like Galen and Byron, but he's real
good-looking with dark hair and light blue eyes and a
smile that can light up an auditorium. Girls fall for him
and write him fan letters like they do Galen. Now and
then one will follow him around mooning, sending him
notes and flowers, until he takes notice and meets her.
Then when she figures out his elevator doesn't make it
to the top floor, she drops him quick. It hurts his feelings something awful.

Lindsey doesn't get the way his mind works. One
minute he'll be pretty normal. And then with a little
stress he'll revert, can't talk except something sounds
like baby talk. He'll think of something, remember
something, and get agitated. One time out of the blue he
told her, "Galen is my *real* brother. One time Galen
give Griff a bicycle. 'Nother time a brown dog. Byron
he kill that dog, mash his head with a rock and say
Griff tell, he beat him up. Mama thinks Griff done it.
She scold. Sometime Byron beat him up anyway. Now
Griff bigger'n Byron."

They've been letting him drive at night when there's
not much traffic. He's real careful and can outlast anybody. Playing the drums, he's really on.

Jason argues for a *real* musician, but Galen says,
"Griff's got music in his veins." And gives Griff a run
at every performance. Griff goes wild and takes the

crowds with him. He's a real happy drummer. Drums
with his eyes closed and that chin-up smile. Galen says,
"He is a man possessed."

"Possessed by what?" Jason grumbles. If you ask
Lindsey, Jason is pure-D terrified of Griff.

Galen, he can play anything with strings. Kylie said
he could play a string mop if they handed him one.
They handed him a ukulele when he was four and he
played it. That floored them. And when they handed
him a banjo, he played that too. By the time he was ten,
he could pick up a mandolin and go wild with Blue
Grass. Blue Grass is the only music left that lets the instrument do the prancing while the picker holds still.
That's when they knew he was some kind of freaky ge-
nius.

Kylie said what did they expect, the boy's from picking families on both sides for generations back.

Galen once told Lindsey if she got up real close to
Kylie, she'd see dollar signs in his eyes. So she climbed
up in Kylie's lap and grabbed him by the ears and gave
him a Judas kiss for the sake of a look. All she knew
was, he reeked of sour mash. No dollar signs in his
peepers.

"Just deep black holes," she told Galen with a shud-
der.

"Right," Galen said. "And you know what a black
hole is, don't you, Lindsey-Woolsey? It's a mysterious
sucking monster that swallows all the energy and leaves
a vacuum in its wake."

She rolls up on her knees and parts the drapes and
looks out. The Indian men are over there again under
their tree. Or maybe they're different Indian men. She
can hear the soft grunt of their voices talking the Indian
language. The cottonwoods out there are poplars. Poplars are short-lived trees, not like the hardwoods back

home. But the Indians' tree looks ancient. Hoary. It's a word they learned in English. Miss Elmwood, the English teacher, makes them learn words in poems if they don't know them already. When it came time for spelling it, Jill Estes stood up and spelled it *w-h-o-r-e-y*. The class cracked up.

As soon as Galen gets back, she plans to tell him what Byron is up to. She's told Byron she will do it. Maybe that's why she hasn't heard from him since yesterday. Good riddance.

But if she tells on Byron, she'll have to confess her part in it. The thought makes her sick to her stomach. So okay, she swapped feel-ups with him that one time. Just curiosity and then, Yuck!

If she hadn't been sent to the stupid girls boarding school in Memphis, she'd have learned all about that stuff without the help of Byron. Anyway, just that one time she learned all she cares to know.

She knows animals only do it once in a while, for the sake of puppies or kittens. But her roommate Mary Beth Hale said people do it any old time they feel like it. Lindsey finds that disgusting. Mary Beth has lots of older siblings who tell her things. Lindsey thinks they are pulling Mary Beth's leg.

Today is Friday. Tomorrow is Saturday and he'll be down off the mountain.

"Come here to me," she whispers close to M'lindy's ear, which twitches with annoyance. She picks up the soft little body that goes limp in her arms, and holds M'lindy face-to-face. M'Lindy won't look at her, just looks straight ahead, with her ears out sideways. It gives her an Oriental look. But she doesn't squirm to get down.

"You're the greatest," Lindsey tells her. "You know that?"

The same ear twitches.

"I know you're listening. I will never go off and leave *you* alone. Not ever. That's a promise."

3

She's never seen anybody die before. She sits back on her heels rocking the body. Then overcome by the sense of danger—bears are drawn to the scent of blood and there's blood everywhere, she's covered with it—she feels something behind her. In terror she turns.

But there's only the silent meadow, untouched, as if nothing at all has happened. But the bear could be back in the aspens, or lurking in the low growth fringing the meadow.

She unsnaps the sheath of her hunting knife. She's never sure why she brings it. Sometimes she hacks up fallen branches with it for fires. But more often they are so blanched and dried by the sun they break easily over your knee. She's comforted by the feel of the knife's heavy hilt.

Maybe the bear is rabid. It didn't seem rabid, but what does she know? A big cinnamon bear, a variety more likely to avoid humans than seek them out.

The body lies limp in her bloody arms. The torn, blood-soaked denim shirt is not from any dry-goods store. It looks expensive, with little useless pockets high up on the sleeves, some fashion designer's idea of ranch wear. The belt is elaborately tooled with squash blossoms and vines, and the big silver buckle is sand-cast Navajo. The bloody jeans are definitely designer, and they fit so tight that going through the pockets is no simple matter.

Her gingerly search turns up a set of car keys, a scrap of lined paper with numbers on it, and a crumpled dollar bill. No identification. She tucks what she's found into a deep pocket of her shorts and presses the Velcro closed.

Laying the body gently back, pillowed on her rolled-up sweatshirt, she looks at her watch. Time has passed. No way can she take the body back down the trail with her. But how can she leave it up here for the bear?

The ledge runs maybe a hundred yards before it joins the ridge, and the rocky scree stretches in places as much as thirty feet from its base. She straightens the body as well as she can, with the arms close beside it. Then she drags and rolls up the biggest rocks she can move. Plenty lie at the base of the cliff, cracked loose and tumbled by alternate freezing and thawing. She circles the body with them, then takes her sweatshirt from under the bloody head and places it gently over the face and torso. The Mimbres people covered the faces of their dead with burial pots. The sweatshirt isn't much, but it's the best she can do.

She covers the body with the flattest rocks she can find. Working fast now, she piles on smaller stones, at the same time asking herself, Why bother? If the bear came back, he could dash the rocks off like pebbles. But compelled to do something, she piles on more stones till the body is covered.

The job done, she finds, too late, she has buried not only her sweatshirt, but also her T-shirt. No matter. She'll retrieve them later, when she comes back with help. Returning to her backpack she digs out the towel and her clean flannel shirt, crosses the meadow, and washes herself and her bloody *panhuello* in the stream, anxiously watching for the bear. The shirt's warmth is welcome after the cold snow water.

Back at her pack, she satisfies her thirst from her water bottle. She could go faster down-mountain unencumbered, but leaving her pack up here goes against all the tenets of backpacking. You never get caught in the mountains without your gear. And left up here, the bear might destroy it with a single swipe. It's expensive equipment.

But she has to hurry. She leans the backpack against the face of the cliff and puts rocks against it. It'll provide little scent if the bear returns. And she should be back with help long before nightfall.

Rushing now, with a final look at the burial mound and a silent promise to the body in the scree, she plunges down the trail. Where it hairpins for a gentler descent, she leaves it and tears straight down through the trees, slipping and sliding on leaves, and that way cuts the distance wherever she can.

But she's making an awful racket. Skidding to a stop, she listens without knowing what she is listening for. The woods are silent except for the birds and her own quick breathing. She rushes on, finds the trail, follows it till it hairpins again, then leaves it and cuts straight down through the woods. Her plunging footsteps are noisy in the leaves. She skids to a halt again, listening.

Could what she heard be the bear? But she knows better. If the bear were following her, it wouldn't stop when she stopped. It would take that opportunity to close in. And a bear wouldn't be silent. It would be snuffling, making those little short growls in its throat as it lumbered toward her.

She peers behind her up the mountain. Any other time, she'd be overcome by the beauty, but now the view up through the aspen forest is eerie. The white trunks could easily hide—what? Nothing, she's just spooked. What she's heard has to be nothing more than an echo of her own running footsteps in the leaves. That or her imagination.

She plunges on, low to the ground, springing with her knees bent to ease the strain of the descent. She's halfway to the bottom of the arroyo dividing Forest Service from Indian land, heading back to where she parked the rig, when she sees him. He's standing on top of the opposite rise looking down at her, his hair pulled back and tied with a thong. But she doesn't need that to identify him as Pueblo.

He can't have been following her. He's ahead of her and on the other side of the arroyo. Why isn't he back in the village, getting ready for San Geronimo? What's he doing here?

He'll soon be asking her the same question. She starts back up to the Forest Service trail. But, dammit, she needs help, it's what she's come down after. She raises a hand to call out to him, but he's disappeared down the other side of the hill.

Now what? Follow him onto Indian land? She'd be trespassing. But under the circumstances . . .

She hears it again. This time she hasn't moved. Is her imagination playing tricks? But something as little as a mountain jay scratching for a worm could make that racket in the leaves. She races down the Forest Service trail, no longer so steep, and in time comes to a jeep track and finally a county road. Damn. If she'd taken this route up, if she hadn't trespassed onto Indian land, the rig would be down here waiting for her.

She passes a melting adobe ruin, then a weathered barn, and comes finally to a farmhouse set back off the road. She crosses the colorful flower border and pounds on the door. No answer. She rounds the corner of the house and peers in a lace-curtained window. Through a door into what seems to be the kitchen, she makes out a wall phone. She could break in and call, but who would she call? She hurries back to the road.

A little way below her, somebody is standing beside a green pickup parked on the shoulder.

Out of the corner of his eye, through his dark aviator glasses, he saw her jogging toward him but he didn't let on. Shorts, long legs, hiking boots, hair chopped off about half an inch from her head. Forest Ranger Victor Cappabono liked his women shapely, with long hair and plenty of makeup, as if they worked a little at pleasing. He particularly liked them a good bit shorter than he was, so they had to look up to him. This one running down the road toward him was as tall as he was.

He went on doing what he was doing, which was jotting his time and location in his log. He could hear her panting as she jogged up. She eyed the insignia on the door of the truck.

"You're Forest Service."

"How'd you guess?"

"A bear's attacked somebody up in the meadow," she said. "I've come for help."

He tossed the clipboard and ballpoint back through the window. They landed on the seat and the pen rolled off and fell among squashed paper cups and crumpled paper napkins on the floor. "Bears in these parts don't attack nobody. This ain't Yellowstone," he said without looking at her.

For a moment she was silent. He thought she considered arguing. But she said, "I'm no expert on bears. I'm telling you what I saw. Somebody's dead up there."

He let his eyes move slowly down her. See what she'd do with that. She didn't do anything but look straight back at him. He didn't care for that look. He let his eyes stray to the alfalfa field beside the road, recently cut, combed in swathes that rose and fell over the contours of the land. He reached through the truck window for his cellular telephone, took off his dark glasses, and dialed.

"This Cappabono," he said, turning his back to her. "I got a party says somebody's dead on the mountain." He turned back again, listening, studying her. "How the hell would I know?"

When he turned away again and went on with the conversation, she was left with the impression of eyes like the marbles she shot as a child, glassy and mottled brown and green, set close together in a face shadowed by a stubble beard, the left one drawn slightly down at the corner by a scar that made it look like part of his face was melting. He had on the regulation matching green shirt and pants. Two horses stood patiently in the truck bed, looking bored. One snuffled. The other one started pawing the truck bed. The ranger reached up and cuffed it on the cheek.

He dropped the phone back through the truck window. "Maybe they had a heart attack. Or fell off a cliff."

Was this going to be difficult? Not if she could help it. "It was a bear. I saw it. I scared it off."

The strange eyes studied her. The pupils were as black as pits, but one iris was a good bit lighter than the other.

"You drove it off. A bear was attacking and you drove it off." Pretending to get it straight, but he was goading her. She was determined not to react. The horse snuffled again.

"He didn't come after you." He said it like a state-ment. "You just ran him off with a stick." He was rid-iculing her, looking down now at his toe scuffing the dirt of the road. He had on fringed moccasins. That was out of character. You'd expect boots.

She looked out at the Rio Grande gorge streaking north-south across the desert, not like the river had worn it down, more like the earth itself had cracked open. Beyond it, the sun was dropping steadily into the horizon. It was already mid-afternoon. When the sun went down, it would be cold on the mountain. She was in her shorts.

The ranger said, "Dead, huh?"

"Yes. A young man."

"Somebody you knew?"

"No."

He looked across the field toward the Pueblo village several miles away and hidden by tawny folds of pas-ture like waves in a heavy sea. He sighed. "I got to go up there anyway." He reached through the window and brought up his clipboard. "Wha'd you say your name was?"

She hadn't said. "Gin. Gin Prettifield."

He wrote it down. "Address?"

Did he really need her address? He was eyeing her with a little smirk. She gave him her address.

"Phone number?"

Everything about the man made her hesitate. She gave him her landlady Magda's number instead.

He tossed the clipboard back in the truck, reached be-hind the seat, and took out a leather rifle case. He rolled up the window, locked the vehicle, and rounded to un-latch the tailgate.

The patient Forest Service horses stepped down to the

road. One was a bay gelding and the other a sorrel. The
sorrel was a pack animal equipped with panniers. No
matter, she could ride it. She grabbed the halter.

"What're you doing?"

What did he think she was doing? "I left my gear up
there."

He thought it over, then put his foot in the stirrup and
winced as he swung into the saddle. That explained the
moccasins. The man had bunions. Then, one elbow on
the saddle horn, he looked down, waiting with a little
smile.

Did he think she couldn't make it up on the sorrel's
back without help? To hell with him. She'd grown up
bareback on painted ponies. She grabbed the mane and
swung up and looked back at him deadpan.

While he leaned on his saddle horn watching, she
took hold of the halter's cheek strap and pulled the sorrel's muzzle around toward her so she could unfasten
the lead rope. She looped it around the sorrel's muzzle
Indian style.

He watched all this with a little smile, then laid his
reins across the bay horse's neck and turned toward the
mountain, and the sorrel followed.

She settled her bare knees forward of the canvas panniers, but that wasn't going to do it. She lifted a leg
over the sorrel's head. The gelding's ears swiveled as he
tried to figure out what she was doing. What she was
doing was settling in sidesaddle. Then, touching her
boot heel to the sorrel's ribs, she prodded him after
Cappabono up the road and into the mountain.

It was getting late. Ben Lopez was hungry. He'd soon
be relieved of his watch, and of the kid as well. He was
more than ready. The day had been boring, nothing go-

ing on. Except the girl. Something had happened up
there on Forest land.

Nothing much going on yesterday, either, except the
singer. They knew all about Galen Hand. He'd been
coming up here for some years now, first with the old
grandfather. Same time each year. Then that summer the
old man died on the mountain, they'd come upon the
boy blinded by tears, nose running in strings onto his
shovel, trying to dig a grave. They'd helped him roll the
old man in a blanket and bury him.

Ben was yawning, picking up his empty beer cans,
when the kid grabbed his arm. They both heard it—
horses, plodding up the Forest Service trail on the other
side of the arroyo and hidden by the hill. Ben crept up
higher and climbed to the crotch of a scratchy piñon
and saw the girl and the ranger. Cappabono, the bastard.
Ben had seen him park his truck over the stream and
open the oil pan and empty the dirty oil right into the
water. Ben Lopez hated the Forest Service. They were
supposed to be guardians of the land, but to the Pueblos
they were more like vandals.

Cappabono and the girl were heading back toward the
meadow. The girl rode without reins but with a nose
noose, Indian style. That was interesting. Something
had happened up there in the meadow or she wouldn't
have run back down without her backpack.

"She's not one of them," the kid said. "If she was one
of them, she wouldn't be coming back up here with any
goddam Forest ranger."

Ben smiled. Now the kid was taking on tribal atti-
tudes. He watched the two on horseback amble up the
mountain. First the bear, then Ranger Cappabono. It
seemed like danger followed the long-legged hiker
around the mountain. He told himself it was nothing to

him. His watch would soon be over and he'd be out of there.

They'd come too far. The grave must be lower down the scree, down there around the bend in the cliff. How could she have missed it? The sun was low, throwing shadows back the way she'd come, and the air was growing chill. She felt the ranger watching, almost idly, as she backtracked, leading the sorrel horse. She rounded the bend in the cliff and stopped, puzzled. She looked up and down the scree.

Cappabono just sat there on the bay horse, looking at her with skeptical eyes that could be smiling, she wasn't sure. "Bear must of come back and stole the body," he said.

Her face warmed up. There was no rock grave and no sign there'd ever been one. She ignored him, moving off, bending over the scree, examining boulders, stopping to touch one, then another, turning them over. "It was about here," she said, straightening, getting her bearings.

Sighing, Cappabono dismounted and slid his rifle out of its case. He walked away, circling the meadow. She went a few yards farther, then turned back, dropping to one knee, trying to read sign like her grandmother had taught her, but there wasn't any.

A wind set the aspens shimmering, their gold deeper now in the failing light. Above them the sky was incredibly blue. She went back over the scree. But it was no different here from the scree above or below. No way she could have missed that mound of rocks. No trace of blood, no strewn rocks the bear would have scattered uncovering the body.

It was turning cold. She had buried her sweatshirt and

her T-shirt with the corpse. And there was no more sign of them than there was of the body.

Across the meadow Cappabono dropped on one knee beside the stream. He picked something up and came back toward her leading his horse, his gun under his arm. He was dangling her T-shirt between thumb and forefinger.

"It's mine," she said. "I buried it with the body. It was soaked with blood." How had it got across the meadow?

He held the black T-shirt by its corners and bent over it in a mocking pretense of inspection.

"So okay," she said. "Dug up right away, blood would wash out easily in the stream."

"Now we got a bear does laundry."

He balled it up and tossed it to her. "And corpses don't bleed."

"He wasn't dead when I found him."

He dragged a package of filterless Camels from his breast pocket, knocked one out, and lit it, shielding the match with his cupped hands, his long face rosy in the flare. He shook out the match and dropped it in the scree. "Okay, let's have it," he said. "What's going on?"

She felt a rush of anger, but her Libra self asked how could she blame him for doubting. "I've told you what happened."

"I don't get it," he said. "What's the point?"

She wasn't going to defend herself.

"Just needed a little attention?"

Don't flatter yourself.

When she didn't answer, he smiled. "So okay. I had to come up here anyway." He turned to the pack horse and reattached the lead rope to the halter. Then he moved to the bay and picked up the reins. "Anything more I can do for you?" He was leering.

She didn't bother to answer.

"Well, so long," he said. "If I come across any dead men hiking the trails, I'll let you know. Don't provoke no vicious bears now, you hear?"

She watched him ride off up the meadow. She might as well have told him she'd found an alien on the mountain, a small bald green person with antennae for eyebrows. When he had disappeared on the ridge, she thought of her pack. What about her gear, had it disappeared too? If it had, she'd be facing a cold, hungry night on the mountain in her shorts.

But she found the backpack where she'd left it. The zipper was partly open. Had she been so hurried she'd left the zipper open? That could let out a whiff of food if the bear came close. She spread the opening gingerly with her fingers and examined the interior. She was a careful packer. Was it her imagination, or were her things more loosely crammed in than she remembered?

She was too chilled to sit there wondering. She dug out her jeans and down jacket and put the jacket on. While her body heat filled the interstices of the down, she dropped her hiking shorts, stepped out of them, rolled them up, and stuffed them in the pack, then stood up and pulled on the jeans.

The meadow was gloomy now, and the gold of the aspens dulled, but the ridge was still bright with the afterglow, and a big magenta wheel rose over the spot where the sun had set. She shouldered her pack, an awkward maneuver over the down jacket, and started to climb. It would be colder up there, but in spite of that and the possibility of wind, she wanted out of this haunted meadow. There was less cover for bears up there, but she was no longer afraid of the bear. What bear making off with a corpse would bother to take her sweatshirt and destroy so carefully all traces of blood and a grave? The conclusion she was coming to was not a relief.

4

By the time Ben made it down the mountain and to the pueblo plaza, the feast day crowd was gathering. Mostly traders from pueblos downriver, who'd come early to be there first thing in the morning to peddle their wares as soon as the footrace was over. Ben looked for his father, the governor.

He saw him up on a terraced rooftop, graying hair braided with strands of crimson felt, watching the goings-on below in the plaza—traders gossiping on the tailgates of their pickups, Anglo townspeople who'd come out to watch the pole go up for tomorrow's pole climb, over there the Spanish priest in his turned-around collar and his hands in the pockets of his black suit, frowning down at the packed dirt of the plaza while his richest parishioner, that Anglo woman, spoke earnestly into his right ear, his good ear. The left had lost its hearing from a shell burst in Vietnam, where he'd been chaplin.

Ben trotted across the bridge that spanned the river bisecting the pueblo north and south. The two would go against each other tomorrow in the footrace. In the cool of the morning, ascending from the kiva in a breechclout, his naked torso daubed with charcoal and umber, feather down floating from his shoulders, Ben would race in the relay for the north while others kept watch on the mountain. The object of the race was not winning but giving back to Mother Earth the energy she'd spent on all the growing things in the summer just past.

He trotted across the plaza, past small boys chasing a dog that seemed to be winning the game, dashing ahead, breaking and dodging like a broken-field runner.

The governor watched him approach. He took pride in his son. Ben was handsome—like his mother, Felipe thought, chuckling to himself—and strongly built, like his father; he squared his shoulders with satisfaction. An old man waved up from the plaza. Felipe lifted his hand waist-high, acknowledging him with a habitual gesture like a blessing.

Ben climbed the pole ladder to the rooftop.

"How did it go up there, son?" the governor asked.

"Nothing much doing. One backpacker"—he saw her again—"crossing tribal land. And a forest ranger. The singer went up yesterday but didn't come down yet." Ben planted a work boot on the firewall and leaned an arm on his knee, looking down at the plaza.

The governor nodded. The singer went up there this time each year to visit the old mining claims left him by his grandfather. Upon his return he stopped by the pueblo for a visit during San Geronimo. This year he'd written asking the governor to expect him.

Ben said, "I guess he stayed up there another night. We heard a bear carrying on."

Felipe looked at him, surprised. "Did you see this bear?"

Ben shook his head. "It was on Forest land."

Felipe frowned. Lines deepened in his face. Ben felt rebuked.

"What was he doing, this hiker, on Pueblo land?"

"Probably cutting out the lower Forest trail, avoiding

all the sightseers out for a look at the aspens. They never go very far up the mountain. It was a woman. She was alone."

"She's still up there?"

Ben nodded, seeing again that long stride.

"You must keep an eye on her," his father said.

Maybe he was worried about the bear. The singer wouldn't be much good with a bear, but Cappabono had his rifle with him, Ben had seen it strapped to his saddle in its leather case.

"Something happened up there," he said. "The hiker went running off the mountain and came back with the ranger." He shrugged. "We didn't go looking. They weren't on our land." So why did he sound defensive? He shrugged it off. Hank, who was older, had been in charge up there, Ben only a lieutenant. Hank Sandoz hated the Forest Service as much as Ben did. Hank aspired to be governor one day. Ben hoped that wouldn't happen. Hank Sandoz was riven with personal angers. He was rash, too quick to act. Surprising that he'd been so cautious today on the mountain.

Felipe said, "So. The singer's still up there. I told him that little scrap of land's not worth anything."

"Something or other keeps him at it."

Felipe shrugged, a shrug that said, Go figure an Anglo. "Maybe he's looking for that old lost mine." He chuckled.

"What lost mine?" Beaver wanted to know, coming up the ladder. His head appeared over the firewall.

Felipe looked fondly at the boy climbing onto the terraced rooftop. Felipe was seldom sentimental, but Ben thought he was sentimental about the boy.

"What did your father teach you?" Felipe had asked upon his arrival at the pueblo.

And the kid said scornfully, "He taught me to smoke and drive a car."

It was hard to tell if the kid had loved his father. Sometimes it seemed like he scorned Arnold Martinez, sometimes he defended his memory.

"The Spanish mine," Felipe said. "First they came, these—conquistadors, they called themselves."

Ben had heard it all. From his father, from the lips of the old men telling the people's history, handing it down in the kiva to another generation in the oral tradition of the tribe. He wanted to climb back down the ladder, but he wouldn't offend his father. Instead he watched the movement below in the plaza. Over on the bank of the river, an Anglo guy was looking up at them.

"They came in golden armor flashing in the sun."

That golden armor would flash forever in a sun that never set.

The Anglo on the riverbank was trying to catch somebody's eye.

"They came on horses," his father said. "The people, they had never seen a horse. They thought what they saw—man and horse together—was a single beast."

The kid laughed at the ignorance of the ancestors. Ben felt a flash of anger.

Over by the river, the Anglo in jeans and hiking boots lifted a hand and waved. Ben was sure he had seen him before, but something was different about him. Then he knew what it was. He was wearing jeans, not one of those loud-colored ski jumpers. He was from the ski valley. When Ben had seen him before, it had been in winter and snow.

"The Spanish captain—this Francisco Vasquez, they called him Coronado—he followed the trail of a black scout named Estevan. Some years before, this black slave had gained his freedom by the will of God and"—he chuckled—"the wreck of a Spanish vessel on the Gulf coast of Florida."

No doubt about it, the man on the riverbank was looking up at them on the parapet, and his father was looking toward the riverbank. Ben saw the governor, without a pause in his story, hike his head in greeting. "This Estevan," Felipe said, "the people took him in because he was some kind of a natural wonder. They had never seen a black man before."

Ben sidled to the top of the ladder and started down.

"When finally this Estevan wandered south to Mexico City, he spread rumors of cities of gold to the north. That captured the Spanish imagination. That one— Hernando Cortez—he told Montezuma that his people longed for gold because they had a sickness of the brain that only gold would cure."

"I don't get Montezuma," the kid said. "First he gave them a lot of gold, then he let them defeat his armies when he outnumbered them a hundred to one."

Ben's father only smiled. "There is a legend he was born here."

"Gimme a break," the kid said.

No matter how many times Ben heard the story, it was always compelling—the Spanish arriving in that golden armor, feather plumes waving from their helmets, and two years later staggering back to Mexico sick and in tattered rags. But in time they returned, and brought with them wives and children and cattle, and Franciscan monks to convert the Indians. Those they couldn't convert, they maimed or killed. They made slaves of the others to build their churches. But a cacique named Popé, from San Juan Pueblo, hid out here in this village and hatched a plot to drive out the Spanish. On Black Mesa, Popé met with leaders summoned from all the northern pueblos. He gave every man a rope with a certain number of knots in it to take back to his village. Each morning when the sun rose, they untied one knot. On the day they untied the last knot, the Pueblos rose up and drove the Spanish back into Mexico. That was in the year 1680.

But the Spanish settlers had found gold in these mountains. The priests—the Franciscans and the Jesuits—were mining it at the time of the uprising. After driving them out, the people hid the mine shafts, filled them with rocks and dirt, and let the brush and trees grow up till all trace of them had vanished. Till this day, those old mines had never been found, which was as the people wanted it, for other tribes had lost their lands when oil or uranium was discovered under the soil. Miners and prospectors had been searching all these hundreds of years since. A man named Virgil—Ben felt sure it had to be the Spanish name, Vigil—found a document in an old church at Guadalajara in Mexico that said by 1680 millions of dollars in silver (some versions said gold) had been taken from the Taos Mountains.

Ben started across the plaza. Josie would still be out at her garden plot beside her father's pasture, drying vegetables, stringing *ristras* of chilis and garlic buds. She had dried apricots from her orchard early in the summer, and put up jars of fruit preserves.

He wondered if the stories of the mines were true. The Spanish word *minas* may have been translated as "mines" but it just meant something like "prospect" or "occurrence," in the mining sense nothing more than "promising."

Still, an old magazine published in Las Vegas, an hour's drive away, had carried a story in the late nineteenth century saying that records of the old Taos church showed the priests had collected ten million in tithes from a single mine on the mountain.

Maybe the old men of the tribe had been told, generation after generation, the location of the mine. Ben would never ask his father what he had no right to know. The singer's grandfather had panned for gold on those old claims every summer during the Great Depression, and found enough to feed his family. Its value then was sixteen dollars an ounce. Now it's astronomical. But panning in the stream was one thing, a mine was another. If the mine was what the singer was looking for, which Ben doubted, he would never find it. The singer had little real knowledge of the mountain. And besides, Ben understood he was already a very rich young man.

He walked past the gringo in hiking boots, a young man with his hair in a ponytail. Ben recognized him as one of the ski valley men who shot off guns to shake the cornices loose and bring down avalanches when no skiers were on the mountain, to avoid accidental deaths in the snow. As Ben passed, they looked at each other. The man from the ski valley smiled. What was he doing here?

Ben looked back at the roof and saw his father come down the ladder and head for the man on the riverbank. He thought of loitering, watching to see if they talked. But that would be dishonorable.

Right after the Civil War prospectors, including Kit Carson, found some gold near the Hondo, the river flowing out of the ski valley, a lot of claims were staked. They put up a stamp mill and started mining, but the ore was in clay, and the clay clogged the stamp mill and ruined it. Ben always laughed at the string of disasters plaguing those eager miners as if something threw monkey wrenches in all their eager greed. A man named Fraser seduced Eastern investors with glowing reports of gold and silver. A town named Amizette, for somebody's wife, soon boomed in the Hondo canyon. Surveyors, engineers, preachers arrived. Some ore assayed $480 a ton, which would be wonderful even now, but the rich ore was spotty. By 1894 Amizette was a ghost town.

Then Fraser found copper underneath the gold and brought in British and French investors and built the mill and put men to work cutting three hundred thousand feet of lumber to build a smelter in what was now the Taos Ski Valley, then called Twining after a New Jersey investor. The mill worked, the ore was rich, but when it got to the smelter it stuck to the cauldron, freezing up the works.

Ben walked past *hornos* where women were baking bread for the celebration, sliding it out of the ovens on their wooden paddles.

When Fraser feuded with Jack Bidwell, one of his partners, and took a potshot at him, Bidwell went for his Winchester and, while Fraser aimed his smoking pistol, shot him between the eyes.

Ben found it all laughable. Anglos and their greed! He shook his head over mining law's concept of "the prudent man," which held that if "a prudent man" invested or staked a claim or mined, then by law it was a valid claim. But anybody who'd get into mining could not in his view be a prudent man.

He knew Felipe was under pressure to enlarge the pueblo's economic base. Some of the pueblos downriver—San Juan, Tesuque, Pojoaque and others—had opened gambling casinos and were raking it in. Santa Domingo had allowed a discount shopping mall to be built on land that abutted the highway to Albuquerque.

He knew the Sandoz faction was pressing for a casino. Others said it would be the ruin of their young people.

Ben knew his father had been approached by ski valley people who wanted to clear a ski run that would cross a corner of tribal land, which they would lease year after year for a handsome sum. It was that or blasting away part of the mountain on ski valley land to build the run. They had first approached the singer and tried to buy the old mining claims, but the singer would not part with them. And as the claims could still be mined, they presented a constant worry to the pueblo. The claims' small window on Forest land would provide access. Not only would mining deface the mountain and mean noise pollution, it would ruin the air, pollute the water, and imperil wildlife.

Some of the people wanted the casino, others were dead set against it. Most were outraged by the idea of skiers on their mountain, but Felipe didn't want any part of the mountain defaced by blasting. Any way his father turned, he faced a dilemma, while enemies waited to see him fall.

Ben shrugged off politics. Leave it to the old men. He passed the greased pole in the center of the plaza, raised that morning without the aid of winches. He shaded his eyes and scanned its height against the cloudless blue. Bags filled with favors would hang from the cross arms at the top, along with the slaughtered sheep, trussed up by its feet with its head hanging limp off its slit neck. Tomorrow a *chiffonete* would climb the pole and tease the crowd, making jokes, pretending to lose his balance while the crowd gasped, throwing down favors the crowd would scramble for, and finally the slaughtered sheep. Each year when the celebration was over, the pole was cut off at ground level so the buried butt could be extracted the next year, leaving a hole for the new pole to slide into.

Ben trotted along the dirt path between a goat fence and a crumbling adobe wall, thinking about the singer still up there among the peaks. The singer had been a strange loner as a boy. That first time he'd climbed the mountain alone, some of the men had come upon him before sunup, sitting cross-legged in the middle of the clearing, singing. That's how they started calling him Dawn Singer. That was before they knew him by any other name.

Ben hoped he would come off the mountain before dark. The singer didn't really know the mountain. There was that time years ago when they rescued him up there. He had wandered and been lost without food or water. But he'd had his grandfather's gun, and he shot a deer. He'd heard you could eat the liver raw. But he'd been so hungry he'd also eaten other organs.

When Ben and the hunters found him, he was raging with delirium and fever. They brought him down to the village to Ben's mother's rooms and nursed him back to his senses, finally back to health. Only a kid then, about sixteen, he'd talked wildly in his delirium about the deer he'd killed. It sounded at first like grief for the deer, but then it sounded like he thought, by eating its flesh, he had become the prey.

He'd never told them what he was doing on that little old worthless scrap of land, five claims, about a hundred acres dwarfed up there by National Forest, the ski valley holdings, and the vast holdings of the tribe. And they never asked. That was the Indian way. They liked the singer. Singers were honored in the tribe, along with the drummers for ceremonial dances.

Pueblo boys helped him out with little jobs on the old mining claims. They'd repaired the grandfather's log shack, put on a new roof, and added a lean-to, cutting the trees, stripping the bark, fashioning roof boards with adzes, doing everything the old way, no power tools on the mountain. Other years they'd found the old markers and cemented the rocks.

Afterwards, he would come on down to the pueblo and eat a bowl of chili with Ben's family, who had cared for him that time he was lost and sick. Sitting late in one of the old pueblo rooms lit by the fire in a corner fireplace, he talked excitedly about saving the world. He would write the songs that broadcast the bad news, and they—the people, and the animals, the animals seemed to have a big part in it—would lead the fight to save Mother Earth. The people listened politely. The singer was full of big ideas. Now that he was older he'd quieted down.

Ben passed the big mound that was an old garbage dump. Anglos sometimes came and begged permission to dig it up so they could study tribal ways and write their books, but the Pueblos wouldn't let them. Instead, they appointed an official liar who could answer their questions any way he liked. Thus they protected their privacy.

Up ahead he saw Josie under her *sombra*. She was bending over her wooden bench full of fresh-picked vegetables, slicing them and arranging them on screens, where they would dry in the sun. She had washed her hair. It was loose, hanging in a curtain to her waist. He could all but smell the *yerba* she washed it with.

He came up behind her and clasped her around the waist.

She twisted to him with a smile. "It's you."

"Who else were you expecting?"

He released her and they stood apart, eyeing each

other with pleasure. They had known each other all their lives.

"I am drying our winter food," she told him.

A little thrill traveled up from his groin. She turned back to her work and he stood beside her over screens covered by *ruiditas* of summer squash. She handed him a screen and he hung it from the eaves. He smoothed the hair of her head. It was black and shining. Usually when he was with Josie he thought of nothing but Josie. But now he was thinking of his father and the Anglo from the ski valley.

As if she could read his mind, Josie asked, "So what is happening on the mountain?"

"I don't know," he said. "There are people up there after something."

"Anglos," she said, summing it up for them both.

He nodded. "A good-looking woman with a backpack went up there this morning."

"Good-looking, uh!" She threw a smile over her shoulder at him. "So what are you saying, you might soon be married but you are not dead?"

He put his arms around her and pulled her close, with both hands on her shapely ass.

On the ridge, where she could see down both sides of the mountain, Gin dropped her pack in the open, beside a ring of rocks from some earlier camper's fire. She scoured the slope for storm-strewn limbs and dragged them up, then piled up twigs and put a match to them. It was still bright up here on the rim, though the meadow below was dim. When the fire was going, she set her cup on a rock and waited for the water to boil, then mixed in her freeze-dried stroganoff.

While it reconstituted she unplugged her Thermarest, which instantly inflated, and spread out her sleeping bag. Those necessities taken care of, she settled against her pack with her legs stretched out in front of her and ate her supper. It wasn't your home-cooked meal, but it wasn't bad.

In the thin air at twelve thousand feet, it was easy to wonder if she'd imagined it all. For the first time, she remembered the artifacts she'd taken from the body. She stretched her leg and dug for them in the pocket of her jeans. Nothing there. Was her mind playing tricks? No, she'd been wearing her hiking shorts.

She rolled up on her knees and unzipped her pack, pulled out the shorts, and found what she was looking for: a set of keys on a key ring with a leather flap, a rumpled scrap of lined notepaper with the word "atomic" and the numbers 58 and 71 written on it by someone possibly bracing the paper against a knee. On one of the numbers, the pencil point had stabbed through the paper. The other item was a rolled dollar bill. She turned over the leather flap on the key ring and found a silver disk on the other side with the scrolled initial H on it. The numbers on the notepaper meant nothing to her.

She picked up her cup and ate the last of the stroganoff with her spoon. Before she pulled on her thermal long johns for the night, she put the keys and the scrap of paper into a side pocket of her backpack. But when she spread out the bill to fold it flat, it turned out not to be a dollar bill at all. Rolled that way, only the 1 had been showing. Spread out on her knee, the one was followed by three zeros.

She'd never seen a thousand dollar bill. Who would take to the mountains with that kind of change in his pocket? Had she buried him alive? She'd heard of such horrors. Maybe he'd regained consciousness and shoved away the rocks and escaped his grave.

In that condition? How far would he have gotten? And why in that condition take the time to destroy so carefully all signs of the burial?

The afterglow faded into night. She leaned closer to the heat of her dying fire.

Cappabono hadn't believed her story. Would anyone? Nobody else had seen the body. With a shiver—it was cold on the mountain—she corrected herself: nobody but whoever had moved it and so carefully done away with all trace of it.

That makes two of us, she thought. She scuffed out the fire with her boot.

A jet's landing lights moved silently up there among the stars, heading for the Albuquerque airport. She imagined the passengers in the lighted cabin, finishing conversations with seat mates, tightening seat belts for the landing, their minds in fast-forward to home and friends on the ground. It made her feel lonely. She'd never been lonely on the mountain.

But maybe she wasn't alone on the mountain. She looked uneasily around. Cappabono was up here somewhere. She hadn't thought she would find that reassuring.

Without the fire, the night brightened. The sky was a lacework of stars, many so faint you never saw them unless you were up here where the air was thin and there was no pollution. The planets, crisp and still, looked down with detachment upon the doings of earthlings. Was there life out there? Was the earth unique in the universe, or only rare? She wondered.

She dug out her thermal long johns, ready to settle in for the night, but then instead gathered up long johns, sleeping bag, and air mattress, and made her way by flashlight about thirty yards down the north face of the mountain where she found a relatively level spot and made her bed. She lay there for some time with her head on her arm, confronting a round, shapeless, shaggy creature crouched at the base of a tree that, when she made herself turn on the flashlight, metamorphosed into one of those holly-like bushes covered with frosted blue berries that proliferate in the mountains.

She spent the night dozing and waking to eye her camp up on the rim. She didn't know what she expected to see up there against the starry sky, but whenever she nodded off, she jerked awake to make out again her backpack, leaning lopsidedly. Silhouetted in the deep of night, its only reference the sky and the hard-edge mountain rim, the backpack's size and dimensions slid easily from small to enormous. It became some ancient, tilted monument sagging earthward. And when the wind stirred the flap she hadn't battened down, a dark flag ruffled from its battlements. But at dawn it shrank to its true dimensions, just her scuffed red backpack leaning against a rock. As the sun rose, she fell into a deep, dreamless sleep.

5

He was fond of telling people that J.R. wasn't his name and oil wasn't his game. But whenever he was too full of profit-making schemes to sleep, he'd creep out of bed to keep from waking Miss Eunice and take himself down to the room she liked to call his study and shove an old episode of *Dallas* into the VCR and sit back and enjoy a cigar while chuckling over and being instructed by the doings of the Ewing clan.

His name, C. C. Chambers, derived from his father's everlasting indebtedness to the Civilian Conservation Corps, which he'd claimed had saved him from a life of crime. C.C.'s father had been such a poor boy during the Great Depression that he'd taken to stealing whatever his sticky fingers touched. One thing they touched had been a 1937 maroon Packard convertible with a white canvas top and whitewall tires that everybody else in town knew belonged to the wife of an elderly judge, who, when the boy was brought before him, promised to send him to jail if he didn't sign up for the CCC, so he promptly did.

And was so grateful to what he thereafter respectfully called The Corps that he named his only son Clarence Charley just so his initials would be C.C.C.

C.C. was also fond of saying he might not be a VIP but he sure was an ROT. That's Rich Old Texan, he'd explain, rocking on his heels and tapping the ash off his cigar with his jeweled little finger, much to the embarrassment of his twin daughters Missy and Lissy, both of whom worked hard at being party girls up at the University in Austin.

Missy and Lissy seldom brought their friends home with them to visit unless they knew C.C. was out of town, for he was fond of draping an arm across any female shoulder that presented itself, and, disengaging, patting a lissome rump. The gesture wasn't lascivious, it was just his way, but Missy and Lissy could have gone through the floor.

Still, he was a more than generous papa. Each twin drove her own smart little Mercedes coupe, Lissy's a hardtop and Missy's soft, they eschewed sorority housing in favor of a plush downtown condominium owned by Papa's corporation—Papa himself being the corporation—and Missy, the youngest by fifteen minutes and something of a tomboy, borrowed, whenever Papa had no need of it, the corporation jet and flew their friends to this or that coast for the weekend, staying at the Plaza when they were in New York and at the Malibu beach house of a country-western star and Lissy's onetime boyfriend when they headed west.

C.C. also had a son. He'd told himself it was something he'd always wanted. His first wife had been barren, which had suited him fine at the time as it would only have meant more mouths to feed and he was not yet rich. But by the time he dumped her for Miss Eunice, twenty-five years his junior, he was rich enough to father a battalion.

So after the girls were born, he pestered Miss Eunice till she relented and let him impregnate her again just as she was getting her figure back. He said he'd give her a diamond necklace if she'd present him with a son, and she obliged.

C.C. stuck out his chest at this latest of his achievements and handed out cigars. But as the boy, a pretty little curly-headed thing, began to toddle, and then to walk, he took up entirely too much of Miss Eunice's time, love, and attention, and even became the apple of the eye of C.C.'s own mama, the boy's grandmother, who, till then, had doted only on C.C. So C.C. set out to effectively deball the boy by the age of five. "Look out for the moo cow, it'll getcha!" And off, screaming, ran little Clarence Cody to his mama. "Look out, here comes the choo choo train!" And off would toddle Cody, crying. "Look out for the black man! He eats tender little white boys like you for snacks." And Cody sat down bawling and messed in his pants.

Then at about the time the boy reached puberty, it occurred to C.C. that a sissy son was no credit to him. So he sent the youngster off to military school in the Old Dominion, which was where C.C.'s father had earlier stolen the 1937 Packard convertible and where the hazing would either toughen Cody up or kill him, one.

But it did neither. Cody survived with a loathing of the military that C.C. found unpatriotic, and ambitions to be a dancer. So, instead of sending the boy to college—who needed it? C.C. himself had done all right without it, and girls were different, he liked lavishing things on them, and what else was he going to do with them till they found husbands?—he'd sent Cody to his big spread out in Bandera with instructions to his ranch foreman, a man much admired for his brutality, to make a man of him.

C.C. was sitting behind his desk in the Texas Commerce Tower in downtown Houston. It was a long walnut table desk, antique French and chosen by Miss

Eunice, who often indulged her imagined knack for decorating. Upon it sat a fancy bronze desk lamp with a Tiffany glass shade—which, because of all the big windows, was seldom needed—a green desk blotter framed in mahogany-colored leather with matching monogramed letter opener and pen set, an autographed photo of C.C. shaking the hand of L.B.J., and a picture of Miss Eunice and another of Missy and Lissy sweetly autographed by them both to the absolute greatest papa in the world.

C.C. swiveled around and gazed out at the early-morning reflections off all the glass skyscrapers of Houston. He inspected the vista often, both proud of himself for rising so high in the world—the Texas tower was the tallest building in the state—and at the same time worried that all this glass would knife everybody, himself included, with flying shards in case of a hurricane from the Gulf. He'd heard a hurricane in Galveston would send a twenty-foot tidal wave as far north as Houston and drown the entire population. Sometimes, instead of profit-making schemes, this was what kept him awake at night. Then he'd sleep late, sometimes till almost noon, when Miss Eunice would come in with a frozen daiquiri on a little tray, singing, "Wake up, hon. Here's your fruit juice."

Last night he hadn't slept at all, and he'd opened his office in the Texas tower with his own key at six A.M. It was Saturday and he should have been sitting out under the candy-striped awning on his flagstone terrace, drinking a second daiquiri.

The phone rang. He'd been waiting for it.

"Papa? Papa, look, it didn't go like we planned. I—"

C.C. bellowed into the telephone, "What do you mean, didn't go like we planned?"

"Don't . . . Look, Papa, don't . . . It's not my fault. There was this bad mistake."

"Goddamnit, boy, I told you this was a last chance. You fail this time it's *feenee*, you get that? You better of got what I sent you after."

"Yeah. Yeah, I got them, all right, but, Papa, we been lied to, and that's a fact, and I . . . Oh, God, Papa, I need you to . . ."

"Quit jabbering. I don't understand what you're telling me."

"Look, Papa, I'm in a jam. I never thought I'd . . . Oh, God, I never can get through to you when we talk on the telephone."

"Another jam, is it! Well, don't expect to be bailed out again."

"Papa, Papa, look, I've got to get back up that mountain but, Papa, I need you to—"

"Where the hell are you calling from?"

"I'm in a cabin in Red River, Papa."

"What the hell are you doing there?"

"Oh, God, Papa, I'm . . ."

"Goddamnit, I can't trust you to do one little thing for me. I swear to God if you can't get this right it's the last chance you'll ever get." He thought he heard sniveling at the other end of the line. "Have you been drinking, boy?"

"No! Only a little, but I—"

"Goddamnit, you better bring me back what I sent you after. That or the money, one. Do you hear?"

C.C. heard sniveling again, and "Papa, Papa, listen, Papa."

C.C. slammed down the phone. Why did he have to take care of every little detail himself. Why didn't he have a son who was just like him and could be his first lieutenant? C.C. indulged in a moment of profound self-pity.

When she awoke the room was too hot. She tried to throw off the covers, and panicked to find herself bound. The bed tilted dangerously, like it sometimes did when she'd had too many margaritas the night before. Somebody was shining a bright light in her eyes. She put up her hand as a shield.

It was the sun that was too hot, and shining in her eyes. It was her twisted sleeping bag that had her all tied up, and the slope of the mountain that tilted her Thermarest. She sat up wrapped in the sleeping bag, and looked at the ridge. Up there her backpack still leaned precariously, the sun reflecting off something beside it—her stainless steel all-purpose cup. Which reminded her, she was hungry.

She struggled out of the sleeping bag, unplugged her Thermarest, and made her way up the slope with them draped limply over her shoulder. According to her watch it was late, half past eight A.M.

She rebuilt her fire and put on water to boil while she brushed her teeth and washed her face. Then she stirred in the oatmeal and powdered milk and ate her breakfast. She had pulled on her shorts and was about to thread her loaded belt through the loops when she thought she heard something.

The bear? Or maybe the lively corpse. Whatever it was, it was up the ridge trail, hidden by the rise. Then she made out the clip-clop of hooves. Cappabono. Now that it was daylight, she didn't welcome his presence on the mountain. There wasn't time to shoulder her gear, so she left it where it was and leapt down the slope toward a cluster of cedars twisted and dwarfed by wind off the ridge.

He appeared on the upper trail north, leading the pack animal. He reined in and peered down from the height of the rawbone bay at her smoldering fire. He twisted in the saddle and looked around. She turned her back on him and looked down the slope of the mountain, waiting for him to be gone.

"Hey, Baldy," he yelled—a reference, she gathered, to her new haircut. She'd taken the scissors to it in exasperation, and now it was about an inch long. "You still up here?" His yell echoed among the peaks.

Go away, she told him under her breath.

But he dismounted and walked around. There was her pack. The fire had scarcely died.

Oh, crap. To get rid of him she shouted, "I'm okay. I'm down here."

He turned toward her voice but made no move to leave. She stepped out from behind the stunted trees as if she'd been taking a leak.

He waved, waiting, but when she made no move to climb to the ridge, he laughed and called, "Don't let no bears get you now." And off he went. She watched him disappear down the rim trail south, then climbed back to her gear.

The sun was higher now. No shadows down in the meadow, just the sun-drenched grass and the gravel of the scree. In the glare of the morning sun, the grass looked white, like a thin covering of snow.

She stood there breathing the clean air, looking down on a hawk gliding below her, hunting for his breakfast. She stirred up the fire and drank a second cup of instant coffee. She was in no hurry to go back down the mountain. She stomped out the fire and scooped dirt over the remains, shouldered her pack, and hiked north on the trail, trying to enjoy the scenery and the solitude. But in spite of herself, she couldn't stop thinking.

Midday, back to her camp for a quick lunch and a short hike south on the ridge trail. She didn't go far. She might run into Cappabono resting under a tree.

Events seemed to have destroyed the backpacking trip. It was afternoon when she gave it up and descended to the meadow. Before starting down the mountain, she dropped her pack by the stream. She wanted to wash her face in the cold water and look for her *panhuello*. She'd missed it last night and thought she must have left it here. She was tempted to drink. The ice in the cylinder inside her new water bottle had long since melted. She took the bottle off her belt and dropped it in the stream in hopes of cooling it a little while she rested. Then she stretched out on her stomach, the moss cool under her, and dipped her head in the icy water.

She sat up and let it drip down her shoulders and over her breasts. It was only when she opened her eyes that she saw it, the change in the stream. The streambed that yesterday had been golden sand was now cobbled with rocks.

Amazed, for a minute she registered it only as strange. Then she slowly realized what she was looking at—the stones from the vanished grave. Someone had carried them bloody across the meadow and paved the streambed with them. No wonder there'd been no sign of blood. There was no sign of it now. The stream had washed them clean.

She sat with her arms dangling off her knees. Okay, this definitely cleared the bear. What if she went after Cappabono, brought him back, showed him the rocks?

What would that prove? The corpse had been moved, and the streambed already cobbled when he walked over here yesterday and found her T-shirt. Somebody had been very busy while she crashed down the mountain to look for help.

Then a movement maybe fifty yards below her on the other side of the stream. Her heart went into syncopation. But it was only a shy elk doe peering out of a bank of fern. A minute later a spring fawn emerged from the alder bushes, three or four months old now and already steady on its delicate legs. The doe drank quietly, one dainty leg out in front of her, but the fawn jittered around, nervous, sniffing the air, looking upstream. Then they faded back in the trees as magically as the bear.

She changed her shorts for her jeans and took her time descending the mountain, the birds following out of sight, calling to one another. Something strange about those birds. Their nestlings would long since have flown. She crossed Indian land to the county road, tossed her pack in the rig, backed out of the piñon thicket and turned toward Taos.

No reason to hurry back to Santa Fe. Santa Fe was all pink and yellow and adobe browns, but Taos lay in a green valley shaped like a quarter moon, with Truchas and Wheeler Peaks, the highest in New Mexico, at its horns, both over thirteen thousand feet and capped nine months of the year with snow. No reconstituted dinner tonight. She would treat herself to a real meal in one of the restaurants.

There were too many old pickups on the county roads for her to notice the cherry red mud-spattered Jeep that pulled out from the low piñons and fell in and followed her into town.

6

C. C. Chambers turned off Kirby onto River Oaks Boulevard. In spite of the fact that the sky over Houston had been cloudy all day, and a cloudy sky made him nervous, he'd stayed late in his office in the Texas tower waiting for the phone to ring.

River Oaks Boulevard was divided. It spread out like a fat rich man that could take up all the space he wanted. It ran down to River Oaks Country Club where C.C. was a member, though he never played golf or picked up a tennis racket or got in the swimming pool. He was pleased to think, however, that Miss Eunice took advantage of all the facilities. She played bridge in the morning and afterward had a lesson with the tennis pro, then lunch in the dining room with the girls, followed by a round of golf before coming home to change and return with C.C. for dinner. Miss Eunice just about lived at the River Oaks Country Club. C.C. was still angry with Cody, but it calmed him to think of that red head of hair, those ample hips.

He wound along River Oaks Boulevard past all the mansions, some with grounds so extensive you could barely make out the houses back among the trees. Miss Eunice would be waiting for him. He'd found her behind the perfume counter at Nieman Marcus in Dallas. He'd been shopping for stocking stuffers for his office girls for Christmas, a chore he enjoyed doing himself. He'd known right away she was what he wanted—a flashy looker with plenty of personality and lots of class who laughed at his jokes. And just as important, here was a girl who would appreciate all C.C. had to offer.

Driving with one hand, his cigar jutting up from between chubby fingers, he turned off the Lincoln Town Car's air-conditioning and pressed the button that slid the windows down. He enjoyed taking his time on River Oaks Boulevard, self-satisfaction puddling in every pore. In River Oaks the muggy air itself felt rich. C.C. imbibed it like full-bodied wine. It pleased him to live in the neighborhood of the rich and famous. Yonder was the house where the doctor was supposed to have murdered his wife. Whatever happened to that old boy? Oh, right, somebody shot him before it came to trial. Some said it was the father-in-law, but they never made a case. C.C. heartily approved. He wouldn't hesitate taking a shotgun to any son of a bitch that so much as harmed a hair on the head of one of the twins.

The early morning phone call from Cody still nettled. Too bad Missy was a girl. Lissy was maybe the least bit more beautiful, but the youngest twin was smart and sassy and could do anything. She took after him. But whoever heard of leaving an empire to the management of a girl? She'd get married and it would all go out of the Chambers name.

Most people hoped their children would do better in life than they had, but the idea never entered C.C.'s head. No way in the world they could best him. It pleased him to know all three worried he'd leave everything to Miss Eunice, he doted on her so.

He had time these days for such ruminations. He'd set up little martinets at the head of each of his enterprises so he wouldn't have to deal with them himself.

But they all knew they could be replaced on nothing more than a whim if he so chose, because the board members were all in his pocket. Now and then he'd drop in on board meetings just to keep folks nervous.

The live oak trees, for which River Oaks was named, looked ancient with their gnarled and twisted trunks and millions of little bitty leaves. They whispered to him of old money. C.C. had plenty of them growing at his place. Just now they were moving in the wind. C.C. could do without the wind. When he got home he'd turn the TV on to the weather channel, see what Houston was in for.

But what did the weather people know? He trusted his knee joint more. In World War II, crawling back from the latrines on a snake-infested Pacific island, he slipped and came down on a rock, and he had a Purple Heart to show for it. His story was, he got the knee storming a Jap machine-gun nest. That came from some picture show he'd once seen about a war hero. He'd told it in a Boosters after-dinner address without a whole lot of thought. It struck him later that the picture show was about some hero of World War I and it was a *German* machine-gun nest. Nobody ever questioned him about it, but sometimes it worried him. Newspapers often ran stories about him. What if some lowdown sonovabitch reporter checked it out?

He had never come up with a better idea to account for his knee, and even if he did, some smart-ass reporter was sure to notice he'd changed his story. He jammed the dead cigar dead center in his mouth and chewed on it. As always, he ended up telling himself: If it ain't broke don't fix it.

This new thing had started out as a toy. He'd happened to catch it on public television, a channel he never watched. And it reminded him that years ago he'd taken a flyer at investing in the movies. He only did it that one time. It didn't sit well that all the long-hair boys seemed to be in charge. They listened politely when he told them his idea of a leading lady—redheaded and shapely, a lot like Miss Eunice—then gave him a lot of palaver about the actress they'd probably already hired. Look at her sideways she was shaped like a board.

But having lunch one day in the studio lot's cafeteria, he'd run into this Indian fella, some kind of a washed-up actor, who babbled about something valuable in the Sangre de Cristo mountains around Taos, New Mexico, where the fella grew up. The down-and-out Indian tried to sell him some papers, including this flaking-to-pieces assay he claimed to have bought at a Mabel Dodge Luhan estate sale in Taos.

C.C., his eyes following a starlet to a table across the room, had chuckled and said to the Indian fella, "Okay, I'll take 'em if you'll th'ow in the Brooklyn Bridge." He'd dismissed the story as just a lot of bull, though he gave the fella a hundred dollars for the papers because the poor loser reminded him of his dear old dad and because the papers looked old enough to be worth something.

One of them turned out to be a letter from the Mile High Assay Company of Denver, Colorado, addressed to Augustine Martinez of Taos, New Mexico, maybe the loser's granddaddy. It said, in effect, they were returning the sample he'd sent them because they were principally a fire-assaying company and not equipped to test for anything except base metals and precious metals like gold and silver, and what he had sent them was not in their purview. They suggested he submit the sample to a "full-range chemical analysis company capable of the new spectrographic analysis." What the hell was that? The letter was dated July 25, 1909, so whatever it was, it was probably obsolete.

Another was a clipping from something called *Mining and Scientific Press*, published in San Francisco and dated December 2, 1913. He couldn't understand all that stuff no matter how many times he read it, but he kind of liked what the clipping said about the little boogers.

Rare earths. They'd taken their name from the ancient Greeks—now that was class—who divided all matter into earth, air, fire, and water. Be better off, C.C. thought, if we'd kept things that simple.

He'd just happened to wake up in front of that show on public television, which in itself struck him as odd. How'd it get turned to that channel? Miss Eunice denied doing it and he believed her. She never watched that crap either. He'd always found his success uncanny, like maybe in spite of a little under the table stuff now and then, somebody up there liked him and was trying to tell him something.

He went looking for the papers he'd got from the Indian fella. They were right where he'd stashed them years ago and forgot all about them. "Well-well," he'd muttered, reading them all the way through for the first time.

He'd sent off for a government pamphlet (ordered in his secretary's name, no need to let the government know what he was up to) and read it cover to cover. It was all scientific gobbledygook. He couldn't make heads or tails of it. He comforted himself with the thought that neither could anybody else. And, furthermore, most people had never heard of them. As he understood it, nobody yet had much of an idea what to do with them. Leave that to the brain boys. Sooner or later they'd come up with something. He trusted that the

Man Upstairs wouldn't have put them here if they weren't good for *something*. He knew that one was used as a catalyst in cracking crude. He might soon have the oil boys coming to *him*. He'd chuckled at the thought and chewed on the end of his cigar.

He trusted his hunch. Hadn't he always played his hunches? He wouldn't be risking much, it was more like a toy. But a toy he was soon hooked on. And he could still get in on the cutting edge. Hell, the whole cotton-picking world could soon be turning to C. C. Chambers. They'd say he was a visionary. He could see himself, a full-color full-page picture on slick paper in *Forbes* magazine.

Only seventeen of the little devils. It pleased him to think they were called *rare*. It excited his imagination that they were formed on the beaches of ancient seas and later uplifted into mountains. He looked at a map and found that Taos was in the mountains, and though the high Taos mountains weren't actually volcanic, they looked out on a great rift valley like the one in Africa, where they'd found all the diamonds. A rift valley was a place where the earth's mantle had split wide open and spread, letting all that magma bubble up to the surface in little volcanos all over the place, bringing treasures from the deep. Not the deep cold sea but the deep hot earth.

He'd shot off a letter to the U.S. Bureau of Mines Experiment Station in Reno, Nevada, and he'd summoned Missy home from Austin to fly him up there in the company jet (keep it in the family), and they'd looked out over all the little purple volcanic hills poking up like girlish tits from the torso of the sage desert embracing Taos valley.

"What're we doing up here, Daddy?" Missy demanded as the little jet bounced and slid nose-first down yet another air pocket.

"Research, darlin', research." And he teased her a little. "I thought you were a daredevil, Missy." The twins had dyed their hair honey-blond, and he liked it.

"I might be a daredevil," she said, "but I'm not a dope. Look at that map." She kicked it toward him with her bare toes. Her purple Birkenstock sandals lay carelessly pigeon-toed at his feet. "The air's crazy up here."

One time as kids, she and Lissy had gone up in their little Piper Cub with too many beers under the belt, and Missy did a barrel roll. They'd been flying barefoot, and they lost their shoes out the windows somewhere over Galveston. Their escapades tickled C.C.'s funny bone.

"Maybe sometime you ought to wear shoes when you fly," he told her, looking out over Taos valley.

"It's not my feet I'm worried about."

"One day," he said, "you'll remember this wild ride. Maybe after I'm gone." He wasn't any spring chicken anymore and he liked a little TLC now and then.

But all Missy said was, "You planning on running down to Corpus?"

C.C. chuckled. She was a chip off the old block.

The Bureau of Mines Experiment Station in Reno replied to his letter with interesting news. This mining specialist signing himself R. Jacovity confirmed his hunch that the little boogers were used more and more in industry, that they were cheaper to work than gold because they could just be sold as a milled product to refineries. Let the refineries deal with the hard stuff. He learned also that New Mexico had been a producer in the recent past and, most important, that Japanese industry had purchased considerable amounts in concentration for their electronics industry.

Electronics, that was the ticket. The wave of the future with C.C. riding its crest. He learned, too, that one of them was used in computers and TV sets to make the good red color. Too bad the commies had gone out of style. He could've supplied them with their favorite hue. Heh-heh.

Right down there was where George Bush lived. C.C. slowed and peered in George's direction. Nothing doing, no Bush in sight.

Rare earths. He liked that. He mouthed it, almost said it out loud. It crossed his mind it sounded like there could be a lot more like this one spinning away out there in the universe somewhere. Now that would be some covered-wagon gold rush. To get there first, get in on the ground floor, take up a few claims and strike it rich on yet-to-be-discovered planets.

He jammed the cigar between his teeth and used both hands to turn in at his own winding drive lined with live oak trees bowing before him in the wind like trusted retainers. Nah, he thought, barely perceptibly shaking his head, that wouldn't wash. This here's one of a kind, our one and only rare earth. His chest expanded with unexamined pride.

7

Lindsey cracks the door and reconnoiters. Aunt Glad's out there reading a romance novel. Her glasses are about an inch thick, but she gets these big-print books and glues her nose to them when she's not playing with her dolls. She's got dolls all over her house, standing up on mantles, lolling around in chairs with their costumes flounced out. Orders them from QVC. She's brought a few favorites along with her on the tour.

Griff in one of his jittery states once went into his baby talk and told Lindsey, "Mama she's crazy in love Byron but Byron makes fun behind back, steals doll, pulls out arm, pulls out leg. They on rubber-band things. Griff told and Byron beat him up. Griff bruise all over and broken head and everything."

"Lindsey, is that you?" Looking right at her but can't make out anything at that distance though she's got on her new contacts. "Come out of there, child, and eat a decent meal." Bright china blue eyes like they've been rubbed with Vasoline, maroon-colored hair swept up and squeezed like a mop on top with a tight little maroon-colored garden of curls escaping.

M'lindy tries to shoot past Lindsey's foot, but Lindsey grabs her and slams the door. "You can't be any more stir crazy than I am," she tells her. "I've told you and told you, we are never in one spot long enough for you to learn your way around outside.

"Look at me!" But M'lindy won't. She has one eye that will cross when she's not happy. It crosses now.

"No matter how smart you think you are, you'd never find your way back to the bus if you wandered. You'd be lost again. Is that what you want?"

She puts her down and M'lindy humps her back and reaches out her arms in a shuddering stretch, stretching even her toes, and yawns to show her boredom. Lindsey found her one day when she got off the bus to eat her lunch in a city park. She was sitting on a bench under a shade tree eating a Big Mac when something landed on top of her, scaring her witless. She screamed and shot up and dropped her lunch. And there was M'lindy, gobbling up that dirty Big Mac as fast as she could. She'd no doubt been up that tree trying to catch a bird. The birds probably got a laugh at the skinny kitten trying to catch something that could fly. But she gave up on birds when she smelled the Big Mac.

She was starving and pathetic and she'd stopped cleaning her fur, a sure sign she was on her last legs.

Galen said absolutely nothing doing, but then he gave in. Since the tragedy he couldn't refuse her anything.

M'lindy was full of worms and spewed loose bowels all over Lindsey's jeans and T-shirt on the way to the vet to get her checked out. The vet said she was sick from what all she'd been eating to keep herself alive. But now she is plump and round and particular about her exotic coat, sand-colored with rings in it, sort of like a bobcat.

Where are Cory Lyn and Jason?

Cory Lyn's real name is Carolyn. She told Lindsey in a moment of weakness, then swore her to secrecy. She said Carolyn didn't seem professional enough so she turned it around to Cory Lyn. She is the bass player and Jason plays the steel. Cory Lyn and Jason are married but you can tell she worships Galen and it ticks Jason off. Lindsey can tell from little things. Like, Jason will say, "Let's eat out tonight, sweetheart," and Cory Lyn will say, "I don't know. What do you think, Galen?" when you know Jason didn't mean Galen too. Then if Galen won't go—which he hardly ever will because he gets mobbed by fans—then neither will Cory Lyn. And Jason will pout. Things like that. People get hung up on Galen. Fans in Tucson almost tore him apart.

Lindsey parts slats in the blind. Just a crack, Byron could be around at the back of the bus, looking in at her with that nasty grin. But she hasn't seen hide nor hair of him all day, for which she's thankful. His latest notion is, If Elvis did it, and Jerry Lee Lewis, why not Byron Hand? They both had younger women, he'd explain. Younger women! If Galen knew what Byron was up to, he'd distribute his body parts all over the state of Tennessee.

She opens the window stealthily. M'lindy's ears prick up, every inch of her alert. She sees a bird. The bird is scrunched down in the dirt with its feathers out, wriggling with its wings hanging loose. She quivers her lower jaw and makes that warbling sound reserved for birds and canned tuna fish.

Lindsey begged Galen to take her up the mountain with him this time, but he wouldn't hear of it. She'd slow him down. Her legs would give out and she'd cry to come down. She'd get scared up there soon as it was dark.

Since when has he ever seen her scared? Since when can't she keep up with him? Goes up there each year because he promised Grandpap, old and dying on the

mountain, he'd never abandon him up there alone
through winter snows and the thaws of spring.

Not this time, Lindsey-Woolsey. He calls her that because she is always gathering wool these days. It means
thinking. So what about next year? He said he wouldn't
be going up there next year.

How come? she wonders. What about Grandpap?

She piles up against the pillows again, and M'lindy
climbs on top of her and starts kneeding her legs.
Lindsey thinks of it as *needing*. She suspects M'lindy
was separated from her ma before she got all her nurs-
ing out and is not over it yet. Kneeding is what tykes do
to bring down the milk. When she does it M'lindy goes
into a trance, and always the same rhythm, like music
nobody else can hear.

So the kneeding won't hurt, Lindsey keeps the little
needle-sharp claws clipped with a fingernail clipper.
M'lindy will sit there with her paw in Lindsey's hand
like a lady at the beauty parlor. She has dark eyeliner
and raccoon rings around her tail and real blue eyes.

Lindsey begged to go on this tour. Ginger and Kylie
were all the time touring. When she was little they took
Galen with them but left her behind. He was part of the
act. Opry crowds loved him, plunking on his tiny guitar
and singing into the mike with his sweet soprano voice.

But she's had enough. She's discovered on this her
first and only trip that she doesn't like it at all. And she
just can't warm to the southwest part of the country.
The Indians are all right, but her nose is dried out, and
her skin's got flakes. Everything out here is in the distance, not like at home where you can almost reach out
the window and touch the trees going by. She misses
trees. This landscape looks like it took its clothes off.
But Galen says they have to stick together after what all
has happened.

She used to believe in God and the angels, up until Ginger and Kylie's twin-engine jet slammed into that little low hill, not even a mountain. Then for a while her prayers were like cussing. After that she decided to quit believing in Him. Who'd ever laid eyes on Him, anyway?

After the crash she quit talking, even to Galen, wouldn't open her mouth, wouldn't let anything pass her lips but her own breath, breathing out the bad, breathing in the good, a mystical practice learned from Mary Beth Hale.

Galen begged her to eat, but she went down to a mere shadow of her former self. He hired a lady shrink, who told her she'd taken the blame for the crash on herself because she was mad at them both at the time it happened, which was a lot of who struck John. She just hadn't felt the need to talk. The time had come to figure things out or go under. That's how she'd put it to herself.

What she figured was: what if nobody believed in Him, would He still exist? Like Mary Beth's scientific puzzle about the tree falling in the forest: did it make a sound if nobody was there to hear? Which, Lindsey argued, didn't make sense. The squirrels and birds would hear, wouldn't they?

Still, she was mad enough at Him to give it a try. She blew Him away. Doing without Him was scary till she brought in Nature instead. Nature was a Her.

But she still prays a lot. It's a habit. She'll be in the middle of praying—Let me be pure, let me see snow next winter—and her mind will drift like a leaf on the wind. She thinks she ought to go back and apologize— who to?—but she just drifts on.

She never means to be praying. It just happens. If

you believe in Nature, is it okay to pray to bugs, flowers? The Druids prayed to trees.

The Indian men are back. Maybe different Indian men. One of them squatting out there under the cottonwood has a bottle in a wrinkled paper sack with its neck sticking out. His arms are propped on his knees with his hands hanging in between. The paper sack's in one of them. They both have a pair of long braids down their chests.

M'lindy is purring. Lindsey picks her up and strokes her, and M'lindy steals up over her shoulder and curls there in a ball, all blissed out.

"You're getting too big for my shoulder." She had to quit wearing Ginger's dangly earrings because M'lindy liked to bat them around.

She feels a lot better today. Pretty soon she will have survived Galen's absence. He will have to be back in time for tonight's performance. It'll be a mini. That means just Griff and Cory Lyn and Jason. The board players' and backup singers' bus is already in Albuquerque, and they'll all meet up there in a couple of days, then head for a big one in Dallas–Fort Worth.

8

Gin parked the rig on the plaza and roamed through the shops, fingering Navajo rugs, trying on turquoise bracelets, coveting Acoma pots, finding nothing she could afford but also nothing she couldn't live without. She climbed the stairs to Ogilvie's, walked through the bar, and sat at a table under a Cinzano umbrella on the balcony over the plaza. It was early for dinner. The bar was full of people back in town after a day at the pueblo. She ordered a margarita and nursed it, people-watching: townspeople out for an evening, you could tell by the way they greeted everybody; tourists in the dining room, you could tell by the bags of souvenirs beside their chairs. Even more tourists than usual, because of San Geronimo.

Inside at the bar two Indians—one with braids, the other with his hair in a thong—drank silently. A couple of would-be cowboys teased a dark-haired woman who was clearly drunk. A young man in a muscle shirt sat talking to the bartender and looking around. The muscle shirt disclosed a tattoo on his upper arm, a failed attempt at macho. Its faded colors resembled one of those decals kids plaster on their arms and rub with spit till the backing comes off, leaving a picture. He was watching her. She turned away.

The cowboy with a sandy two-day stubble came out

on the balcony and walked unsteadily to her table. He picked up a chair, turned it around, and straddled it.

"Wanna little company, darlin'?" He grinned drunkenly.

"No thanks."

She looked out over the flagstone plaza where cars circled slowly, and hoped he'd go away. He reached out a paw and dropped it heavily on her shoulder. "Me, I get lonesome, drinkin' by myself."

She shrugged off the hand. It slid caressingly down her back.

Tattoo loomed up beside her table and took hold of the cowboy's collar. The gesture was as macho as his tattoo, but there was something almost fragile about him—fine features, the pale hand with long fingers, even the uncertain way he cleared his throat and said, "Get lost, mate."

The cowboy knocked off his hand.

"You heard what the lady said. She's not eager for your company."

Inside the bar, eyes turned toward the balcony. Nobody sat at the other tables. It was a little chilly. She reached up to brush the insect off her forehead, but it was the telltale vein. She was surprised when the cowboy rose, muttering, turned the chair back around, glared at Tattoo, and returned to the bar.

She felt obliged to say, "Thanks."

He pulled out the cowboy's chair, sat down, crossed his legs, and leaned toward her. The people who'd been watching turned away, all but a Pueblo man with his hair in a thong. He sauntered onto the balcony and leaned against the open French door with a beer in his hand, watching.

"You a native?" Tattoo asked, drumming his fingers on the table. "I been looking for somebody to show me around." He smiled. He had good teeth. One knee crossed over the other and the foot began to twitch. He sat hunched over, looking around, then looking back at her. He was either nervous or hyperactive. "Can't blame the cowboy for hitting on you," he said. "I was tempted myself."

What else did he think he was doing? But there was something false about it. He was trying to pick her up but he didn't know how. And she seemed irrelevant to his endeavors. Maybe he'd bet somebody he could do it. She looked around. The Pueblo brave leaning against the door with a beer in his hand?

She thought of helping Tattoo out, but then she'd be stuck with him. "Look," she said, "I appreciate what you did, but, really, I can take care of myself."

He was instantly still. The smile fell off his face. He looked like he could cry. In spite of his limp, thinning hair, she knew from his girlish complexion and pink lips, either from nature or because he kept catching them in his teeth, that he was very young.

"I'm sorry," she said quickly. "I don't mean to be rude."

The smile instantly returned. He hugged himself like he was cold in his muscle shirt, and rocked back and forth.

"I'm a rancher from west Texas," he said with an attempt at bravado.

He struck her as just about anything but a rancher from west Texas. She was touched by that thinning hair. Before many years, while still little more than a boy, he would be bald.

"Been up to Red River for a little trout fishing."

He was too jittery for trout fishing.

"I'm on my way home," he said. "Got to catch a

plane in Albuquerque, but I thought maybe in the mean-
time you and me could, you know, get acquainted."

He really wasn't good at this.

The Pueblo guy was still watching. Poor Tattoo
would lose his bet. "You'd better be on your way," she
said, "if you've got a plane to catch."

He smiled and his face mottled. "I could be talked
into missing that plane."

"Look, I'm in the mood for a quiet dinner all by myself." Get lost, please.

That quick change again, to a look almost frightened,
so bruised she had to quell the impulse to comfort him.

"Maybe we could, you know, take a walk around the
plaza or something."

She shook her head. "I'd like just to sit here and finish my drink."

That seemed to take awhile to register. He nodded.
Angry, hurt, or insulted, she couldn't tell.

"Like alone, you mean."

He looked uncertain about what to do next. What you
do next, she thought, is go away. He stood up and set
the chair up to the table and leaned on its back with
both hands, straight-arming it, his shoulders up around
his ears, and glanced around as if he hadn't given up
yet, was trying to think of another tack. The Indian was
watching. Tattoo was losing his bet. She wondered how
much.

His mouth worked but nothing came out. Finally he
flushed and touched his forehead in a limp salute.
"Thanks. I mean for being, you know . . ."

No, she didn't.

He turned on the heel of the roping boot that gave
him a few extra inches, and walked stiffly into the bar.

The Pueblo guy smiled at her. She picked up her margarita and moved to the dining room. She ordered

fajitas and sat looking around. She had the startled impression that a young giant in a turned-around baseball cap over at the desk had turned hastily away. It must be the new haircut.

She drove through Ranchos and Llano Quemado on the outskirts of Taos. Dusk was thickening. Nighthawks dived over the sage as she sped up on the long straight stretch of highway toward the canyon. To her right the Rio Grande Gorge looked like a streak of lightning fallen from the sky and lying stretched out for miles, a burned-out cinder, across the desert. Cars coming toward her out of the canyon had their headlights on. By the time she was deep in the gorge and dropping toward the Espanola valley, beloved, she reminded herself, by Willa Cather half a century and more ago, the cliffs were hard-edge silhouettes on one side of the highway and the river a black chasm on the other. The bright corridor of sky between was lit by stars.

There wasn't a whole lot of traffic, so she noticed the headlights bearing down behind her. Muttering, she slowed on a short stretch of the twisting two-lane blacktop to let him pass. The Rio Grande ran at the bottom of the embankment on her right. Up ahead the rapids picked up light from the sky.

The car pulled out to pass, then abruptly cut in front of her. She slammed on the brakes and spun the wheel. The rig swerved off the highway and bounced roughly down to the drop. The aging seat belt caught too late. Flung into the steering wheel, she braced herself for the plunge.

But the car dipped and rocked and dipped again and stopped. Stunned, she lifted her head and swiped at her nose and brought away fingers sticky and wet. Dazed and disoriented, she struggled to hold onto consciousness.

The car moved, its rear end reared, throwing her forward. God, it was going. She struggled to free herself from the loose seat belt. The car swung sickeningly. Was she in the current? It was sinking! But while she held her breath, unable to scream, the rig settled again.

Why couldn't she see? The dashboard lights were still on, she could tell that much. She put up a hand. Blood in her eyes. She swiped at it with her sleeve. Through a red film she watched the headlight beams seesaw in slow motion up and down over the opposite canyon wall, illuminating rocks and sage. She was not in the water. The rig was hung up on the ledge. It could go any minute. She tried the door. It was jammed. The motor was still running. She reached to turn off the ignition but caught herself in time. She pushed a button on the armrest. Miraculously, the driver-side window slid down. She peered out into the void. The damp night air over the river revived her. The front end of the rig hung out over the drop. Even if she managed to open the door, it hung out high over the river.

What happened next was confused and murky. A rapping she couldn't identify seemed to come from behind her. She was afraid to move. The rapping came again. Slowly, she twisted around. The rear window framed a silhouetted head, a hand that motioned.

She prayed as she fingered another button. A whir, and the rear window moved, stuck a moment, then slowly lowered. Thank God the-twenty-year-old station wagon had once been a fancy automobile.

"Are you all right?" a soft voice asked.

She tried to speak but nothing came of it.

"Hold on," he said. He disappeared into the dark, and but for the moisture-laden air streaming in from the back of the station wagon she might have taken him for an apparition.

He came back scrolling a pale cotton blanket into a roll. He tied one end in a knot. "I'll toss this to you. Grab it and hold on."

The first couple of tosses didn't make it past the backseat. It hurt to breathe. She'd hit the steering wheel hard.

"Turn around. Slowly!"

Obediently, she turned.

"Now up on your knees."

But her knees were too weak.

"It'll be okay. Just take it easy."

Slowly she rose. The rig didn't move. He whipped the blanket like a rope and it snaked forward. She grabbed the knot and held on while the station wagon lurched forward.

"Hold on! Easy! You okay?"

She couldn't answer.

"All right. Come on!"

She had to force herself to slide over the seat back. She made it to the backseat on her hands and knees. She thought the rig moved again. She thought she screamed.

"Hang on! We're almost there. That's right. Easy!" She felt him grasp her arms. "I've got you!" Arms entwined like trapeze artists, they froze while the rig settled. "Okay, *now*!" He pulled, and her legs scraped over the edge of the rear window.

She lay huddled on the ground while the frame of the rig scraped slowly forward over the drop. A shadowy form stood over her. They waited for the station wagon to go. Again it stopped and hung there on the edge.

"Thanks," she gasped when she could speak. "The bastard ran me off the road."

"I saw," he said. He walked over to the rig, reached

into the rear window, and pulled out her backpack. "In case she goes." He set it down beside her.

A noisy truck ground up out of the canyon, heading for Taos. From the truck bed, dimmed by the straining motor, came the sound of voices talking and laughing. As the truck made the turn in the winding road, its lights raked across the rig hanging out over the river.

Somebody yelled, "Whoa!"

In the headlights she had a quick impression of her rescuer: broad, young, something on his neck—the bill of a turned-around baseball cap? or long hair tied in a thong? Maybe Indian. He held out a hand. "Thanks," she said, taking the hand, letting him help her up. "I'm Gin Prettifield."

The truck was rolling off the highway toward them, coming to a stop. Figures swarmed over the wheel wells and leapt to the ground. "What have we got here? *Cabron!* Back up! Back up! The winch, *chingado!*"

Apparently he hadn't quite heard her in the noise. He said, "Pleased to meet you, Ginny Field."

"Who are you?" she called after him as he walked away.

She thought she heard him say, "I am your guardian angel."

He faded into the dark as they swarmed around her, chiding each other in Spanish as the truck nosed down the embankment toward the rig.

Somebody yelled, "Stop!" Somebody else yelled, *"No me chingas!"*

A young man stood in front of her in the headlights with his hands on his hips. His crinkly brown hair, a little long on his neck, peaked on his forehead and joined a short beard wrapping his lips in a soft mustache. Put him in armor and helmet, he could have been a conquistador. "Don't worry," he said. "We'll pull you out. Okay?"

Surrounded by activity, she looked where the guardian angel had gone, but he had disappeared.

Amid the yelling, the winch on the front of the truck began to whine. The rig shuddered. Slowly it slid backward, scraping on its frame till the front wheels stuck on the lip. The whine of the winch rose to a keen. The front tires turned, the rig backed, bounced, and sat rocking with all four wheels on solid ground.

A whoop went up. Someone yelled, "Let's see will she start!" and climbed in the driver's seat. The motor ground, stopped, ground again. Someone else yelled, "Let me, Emilio!" and shoved into the driver's seat. The motor ground again.

"Ven paca!"

"A puralé!"

Up went the hood. They all bent over the motor like voracious eaters at a picnic table, elbows in the air, arguing noisily in Spanish.

"*Cabron.* Some kind of a thing knocked loose."

"Vêté. Vêté." The low voice brought instant quiet. They all straightened and looked toward the truck.

The driver stepped down from the cab. "I 'ave got a chain back there somewhere. One of you, go find it." The head snapped with authority toward the truck bed.

"*Sí.* Go find it, Orlando."

"*Celle te la boca.* Find it yourself!"

"*Silencio*! Get the chain, Emilio," the driver said, tall and broad in a red-and-black check flannel shirt, bending to relight a thin cigarillo. The shirt was tucked into jeans, and the jeans into rubber knee boots.

"You heard her! Hop to it, Emilio!"

Gin squinted through the dark at the figure silhouetted by the truck's headlights and planted like a tree.

"I got it!"

"Hitch 'er on!"

"Back 'er out on the highway, Soledad!"

Soledad. But they couldn't all be her sons, they were too close to the same age. The slatted sides of the flatbed truck were up. It was filled with firewood. They'd been on a wood run. The driver swung easily into the cab but left the door open, gripping it with one hand. The winch groaned. The truck backed and the rig moved.

One young man stood in the middle of the highway directing traffic with a flashlight while the others pushed the station wagon back onto the blacktop and undid the chain. The truck rocked, rolling slowly back onto the pavement and around to the front of the station wagon.

Two woodcutters fell down on their backs, arguing and shoving. The chain got reattached to the rig's frame while traffic eased around them. A convertible driver cursed. A low rider threw a finger. The woodcutters shouted back insults.

The conquistador took her arm. "Come on, let's go!"

All the way into Taos, over the noise of the motor she could hear them talking and laughing. Air rushed in through the open windows, restoring her. Somebody beat on the roof of the cab, and the driver reached into a paper sack on the floor and lifted a can of beer out the window. A disembodied hand came down and grabbed it. The conquistador brought up another can and popped the tab. "Here, drink!" he said, nudging her. "It will calm your nerves."

She took it gratefully. After her fright, squeezed in between the driver and the bearded conquistador she felt safe, almost euphoric.

"Where you want to go?" asked the driver, Soledad.

"I don't know. A motel."

"*Sí*, hokay."

The conquistador reached for another beer from the floor of the cab, but Soledad leaned across Gin and tapped his hand smartly. *"No más!"*

They pulled off the highway across from the Taos rodeo grounds.

"This a good place," the driver said. "My sister's girl Mercedes, she works here sometimes." It was a small motel squeezed in between bigger, fancier ones. "Good eats up there." She pointed to a neon sign up the highway. "My nephew, his place is there, you see?" She pointed toward town with the hand holding the cigarillo to a garage with broken-down cars parked around it. "We tow it up there, hokay? You go see *Tómas*. He will take good care of you. He will fix you up."

But not before Monday, Gin thought.

The bearded conquistador got out and handed her down. The woodcutters hooted and laughed. Somebody dropped her backpack to her over the tailgate.

She looked up into the truck cab at the driver. "Thanks. Thank you," she said. In the light of the motel sign, curly gray hair escaped the knit cap, and lively black eyes smiled down at her. Aries, she thought. "Thank you," she said again. The woman Soledad nodded, and a sudden smile sparked in her eyes and crinkled fine lines all over her face. Then she jabbed the cigarillo back between her teeth.

They waved and shouted, pulling away. She watched them stop traffic while they turned, towing the rig into the garage lot. Several leapt down and unhitched it and, shouting and shoving each other, pushed it into a parking space. They waved in her direction. The truck sped up. They ran after it yelling and, grabbed by their mates, scrambled aboard. Wherever they were going, she wished she were going with them.

The desk clerk leaned on his elbows on the counter, discussing the baseball strike with a state patrolman getting a Coke from the machine. They shook their heads with disgust. "How much more money do they want?" the patrolman asked.

While she filled out the form, she told them about being run off the road in the canyon. The patrolman wanted to know if she'd got a look at a license number or make of the car, but she told him she had not. They shook their heads at what the world was coming to. She paid with her credit card and took the room key.

The rodeo arena across and a little way down a side road was all lit up and a voice came over the speaker system. A slow line of cars streamed into the parking lot.

Good. A rodeo. Maybe she would distract herself. She liked bronc riding. But the banner strung between the gateposts didn't say Rodeo Tonight. It advertised a singer. She'd heard of him. Galen Hand. So okay, she liked country and western. She'd give it a try. It was that or the Gideon Bible.

In the *portál* outside the office, she dredged change from her pocket for the newspaper rack, pulled out a *Taos News* and glanced at it. Whatever the picture on the front page was, she saw two of them. She closed her eyes and shook her head. A mistake. Her head had begun to throb and she was suddenly aware of becoming very sleepy. She folded the paper under her arm and made her way to her room and a hot bath.

The room was pleasant. *Vigas*. A corner fireplace. She tossed the paper on the bed and squinted at the headline above the fold. "Galen Hand, Country Singer of the Year, in Taos Tonight." Funny, the big black headline letters trailed shadows behind them, making them leap out of the page at her.

9

Lindsey is watching TNN. Kylie'd had the four-and-a-half foot dish installed on top of the bus. Galen almost took it off. Galen hates TV because anytime he turns it on he is likely to see himself. She talked him into leaving the dish so she wouldn't get bored. It lies down while they're moving, but she can put it up by remote from inside the bus as soon as they park.

She's hoping for Billy Ray Cyrus, but right now somebody is interviewing The Flying Burrito Brothers, who are making a comeback. She likes Brian, the one from Australia. He calls people Mate. He has long fluffy gray hair now, and a beard. Their new album is "Eye of the Hurricane."

Back at the Brentwood mansion there's a big satellite dish. But Galen's put the mansion up for sale. He's always hated it. Says it was never a home and with all that red carpet and red swag drapes it looks like a funeral parlor. Fourteen rooms, and every electronic device known to man. All the girls at boarding school beg to come home with her for a weekend. The mansion makes her Somebody.

Now everything's falling apart. When this tour ends Galen says they'll pack it in but he won't say why. She thinks it has something to do with the letters he keeps getting from some guy named John Francis.

Everybody's against it. Jason acts like he could just kill Galen. Because of all the money they won't be making.

Money doesn't matter to Galen because, he says, he's got more than they'll ever need. He gives a lot of it to causes. Maybe he's giving money to John Francis. She wonders who is John Francis. That's all it says on the envelope, John Francis. The letters come from a P.O. Box in a town she never heard of in Kentucky. There's one right now in the bedside table drawer. It's open. He's already read it. She feels the urge to read it herself, but she has a sense of honor.

Galen gets bushels of fan mail, but it's funneled through his agent. Not these letters, though, and not the postcards that come several times a year and had Ginger worried before the crash. Nothing on them but a pen and ink drawing of a bear, sometimes standing up, sometimes on all fours, sometimes like a teddy bear sitting on its behind with his feet out in front of him. That's all, except for the numbers, different every time, like 513 or 924 or 1011. It's after the arrival of one of the letters or postcards that Galen takes sudden leave for days at a time. She's sneaked looks at the postmarks on the cards, but they're never the same: Minneapolis, MN, or Scottsdale, AR, or Big Sur, CA.

Up front Cory Lyn is cooking something in the kitchen that smells like beans—Lindsey is getting hungry for some real food—and Jason is talking in this tight voice he gets, sounds like he's squeezing it out of a toothpaste tube.

"I'm your husband, damn it, or have you forgotten? I'll be around when this thing is over, and I might be the only one."

At it again. When he's not mad at her, he's pleading. Jason is heartsick with love but Cory Lyn is rejecting.

Lindsey opens the door a crack, and before Lindsey

can stop her M'lindy shoots out to the front of the bus. Jason scoops her up and holds her in the crook of his arm where she looks like a pathetic prisoner. Lindsey leaves her where she is. Teach her a lesson.

"Where you been keeping yourself, Lindsey?"

She doesn't bother to answer. He knows where she's been keeping herself. She can't see why anybody would take what all Jason takes from Cory Lyn. But she can't blame Cory Lyn. Jason drives Cory Lyn to distraction. She is already in one of the long, flowerdy dresses she performs in. Lindsey thinks she is beautiful with her long, glossy hair and violet eyes. She is putting back on a fingernail she's torn off. Cory Lyn is as sad as she is beautiful.

"Honey," she says to Lindsey without looking up, hair falling like drapes alongside her face, "did Galen say anything to you about maybe not getting back tonight?"

That stops Lindsey cold. Galen has pulled this stunt before. This last year he has been late for more than one concert, to the delight of cousin Byron. And once he disappeared for days and Byron got the break he'd waited for. He's got Galen's autograph down to a T, also his mannerisms. Of course he couldn't carry a tune in a bucket. Outside, the rodeo grounds are already lit up bright as day.

"Because if he doesn't make it we'll have to go to plan two." Cory Lyn looks at her with worried eyes.

Lindsey pretends she hasn't heard. She takes M'lindy away from Jason and tosses her back onto the king-size bed and slams the door, closing M'lindy in. She sniffs a tortilla to make sure it hasn't turned moldy—the bus's refrigeration isn't the greatest—and sticks it in the microwave.

"There's beans," Cory Lyn says. "Aunt Glad chopped

some lettuce and shredded some cheese." She bends
back over the nail and starts painting it with the little
brush. The paint is the color of her eyes. Where's Aunt
Glad? Probably shut up in her room watching QVC for
another doll show. The latest arrived just before they
left on the tour, a doll named Savannah that looks at
you with these sincere eyes.

Lindsey takes the tortilla out of the microwave and
piles on the ground meat and taco mix from the skillet.
She lets the beans alone. Beans give her cramps. She
drops on some cheese and spoons salsa along the top
but skips the lettuce. She can't see any point in lettuce.

Jason grumbles, "Griff better get back here pronto.
I'm sure as hell not lugging up them drums." Jason is
tan—tan skin, tan eyes, tan hair, tan sideburns. He is the
one who mostly drives the bus. Him and Griff. If Jason
and Griff are both bombed out, not enough sleep,
they'll let Byron do it but only with a wide-awake co-
pilot, sometimes Lindsey, sometimes Cory Lyn. No telling how many times they've yelled at him, "Pick a
lane, Byron!"

Lindsey says, "I haven't laid eyes on him."

Nobody's seen him. Galen's not back, and neither is
the little Japanese pickup they drag along behind the
bus with its front wheels up on a trailer. The two of
them left in it to go to the mountain, and they ought
to've been back long before now. You can feel the ten-
sion in the bus.

Griff loves Galen, always has, ever since they were
children and Galen took up for him. Byron is ashamed
of his slow brother, and Griff can't help but know it.
His face goes red whenever Byron teases him, which is
often. It's supposed to be funny, but there's always a
streak of pure meanness in it. If Galen's around, Griff
will defy Byron, but let Galen be out of sight, Griff re-

verts to being Byron's slave. Lindsey wishes they could leave Byron at home.

"And where the hell's Byron?" Jason asks.

Cory Lyn says scornfully, fanning her hand and holding it out to look at it, "Don't worry. He wouldn't miss it for a million bucks."

Lindsey takes her taco back to the bedroom, locks the door, and piles up against the pillows to eat it. M'lindy climbs up her and goes after her share. Lindsey swings the taco out of reach. "You know you hate salsa."

On TNN here comes not Billy Ray Cyrus but Neil McCoy, in a pink shirt and white cowboy hat and bolo tie full of turquoise, singing one from his album "No Doubt About It." Out front, Cory Lyn and Jason are talking about plan two. Lindsey doesn't want to hear it. She turns up the volume. She likes Neil's sweet songs best.

They've announced Cassandra Vasik will be next. Cassandra Vasik is from Canada. She has these pale gray eyes and long black hair and wears a lot of lipstick. Lindsey likes Cassandra Vasik. She could do without the lipstick.

She polishes off the taco and wipes her fingers on her T-shirt, M'lindy watching every move. "Quit it," she tells her. "Do I go after your tuna?" M'lindy droops down to the end of the bed. "Now don't get an attitude."

Lindsey parts the drapes to see if the little truck is back, but all she sees are some boys playing Territory over there under the lights. One of them stands the blade of his pocketknife on the pad of his index finger and flips it off. It sticks up in the ground. Cool.

She tells herself she isn't worried yet. Galen is always doing things like this—like taking long walks by himself and leaping straight up on the stage in his old clothes right at the last minute and grabbing the guitar.

It's enough to give you heartburn. But at times he has
to get away. That's what he's told her—he just has to
get away. Sometimes it's for days. She suspects he goes
to see this guy John Francis. For some reason, she's
scared to ask him about John Francis, just eyes the letters when they arrive and wills him to say something.
He never has.

Neil McCoy's getting a lot of applause. Now here
comes Cassandra Vasik in a funny hat. While Cassandra
Vasik chats with the MC, Lindsey goes on worrying. It
must be a long climb up that mountain. He's not in
shape. Doesn't take care of himself.

But you can say one thing about Galen, he's loyal.
He didn't always know how he felt about Ginger and
Kylie—he was of two minds about all that performing
when he was a little kid—but he adored his grampa
Lester. Lester Hand. This yearly thing is for him.
Grampa was a singer—fiddler, too—in his time. She
wonders does Galen still sing to him up there. Tonight
he'll be sure to sing that old Stonewall Jackson favorite,
"Me And You And A Dog Named Blue," because
grampa loved it. Also "Waterloo." Though both songs
are completely at odds with Galen's style.

Stonewall Jackson is a country-and-western legend.
Older now, and sort of stout. But he showed up in
Nashville as a young man with nothing but a pickup
truck and a sackful of songs. Kylie's generation.

With all the songs Kylie wrote and sang, let him get
a few beers in him, all he'd sing was, "It ain't gonna
rain no more, no more, Oh it ain't gonna rain no more.
How in the heck can I wash my neck when it ain't
gonna rain no more?" She can hear him now. They told
her it was impossible, you can't remember that far back.
But she clearly remembers Kylie holding her up over

his head and her laughing, arms and legs going like a swimmer's, and looking down on his thinning hair.

She tries to think what she wants to be when she grows up. Not a singer, not on your life. She would pure-D hate performing at anything in front of an audience, and crowds give her claustrophobia. Besides, in spite of generations of country singers behind her, like Byron she can't carry a tune.

Galen's songs grow stranger all the time, the lyrics no longer about love lost, love found, love gone wrong, and similar heartfelt subjects. His songs get farther and farther out. Whatever's happening inside him's got her worried.

She hums, then watching Cassandra Vasik and the MC—talk talk talk—sings under her breath,

> The stars are cold
> looking down on us
> there is no heat
> in star dust.
>
> The ice age comes
> the flowers go
> to frozen seeds
> beneath the snow.

The tune's haunting. She hears it in her head, though she never can get it right. It's lonesome and it's pretty, but it's sure not country, and it's sure not western, and she doesn't have a clue what it's about. She thinks of the letter in the bedside drawer. John Francis's handwriting on the envelope is an even, neat Palmer Method.

She knows clearly how she'd felt about Ginger and Kylie. She'd loved them to death.

Cancel-cancel!

She got that from Mary Beth, who is spiritual. Mary Beth says it is the belief of the church her parents attend that your thoughts are what cause whatever happens to you in real life. But if you *accidentally* think something you don't mean, you can say cancel-cancel and it's as if it had never been.

Of course she'd loved them, Ginger and Kylie. They were her folks. Maybe she didn't love them all the time. Sometimes when they were actually staying at the mansion, they'd summon her home from school for a little time together, exams or not. And she'd long for them to be off again. Because Kylie would drink and Ginger would yell at him about it. But Kylie drank because of all the pressure. He told her that himself. He said he was under a lot of pressure. But Ginger said touring calmed her nerves as she had to be moving to keep up with something inside her that was always on the run.

Lindsey loved them best when she saw them on TV singing heartwarming songs full of love and family values. When she heard Ginger singing one of those old-timey songs, Lindsey knew she was thinking of her great-grandma Harkin. Ginger had been orphaned at birth. She'd lived with her grandma. Then she'd gone to live with great-grandma Harkin up at Sojers Gap after her grandma, middle-aged at the time, ran off with a drummer. Lindsey thought a drummer like in a band, but Ginger said it was some kind of a salesman.

Great-grandma Harkin lived up at Sojers Gap in her house that Ginger said had never known the touch of paint. Just weather-gray logs with a deep front porch behind shades of morning glory vines. "It just set up on cairns of stones," Ginger would say, wonder in her voice and a faraway look in her eyes, "and the chickens ran around pecking underneath. And morning glories all along the path to the privy." A two-seater, Ginger said, from the days when great-grandma still had her children at home.

"I ran away wanting to see the world," Ginger told her sadly. "I didn't know then that those days at Sojers Gap were to be the happiest of my life."

Lindsey, just a little thing then, had asked her, "Did the Sojers live up there, too?" Otherwise, she thought it might be a lonesome place.

Ginger threw back her pretty head and laughed. "Aw, honey, you kill me. They weren't a family, they were *sojers*. You know, Bang Bang! They went off to fight the redcoats with their old flintlock hunting rifles." And some of those old ghost soldiers climbing the trail through Sojers Gap on their way to war, were, Ginger said, their own flesh and blood.

Ginger told Lindsey everything she could remember about that house with the chickens running loose underneath, and the two-holer privy, and how great-grandma Harkin, whenever she stopped to rest, flopped one of her geese upside-down on her lap and told it to hush up complaining, and she'd pluck the down off its underside. That's how she made her feather beds.

Lindsey pictured everything in her mind. Ginger told it while they were piled up in her and Kylie's bed. The bed was on a dais, which meant it was on a built-up platform. You had to step up even to get to the bed. And it had a padded pink satin headboard and a flouncy rose canopy that Kylie grumbled about, but he slept under it every night he was home.

When he wasn't, Ginger let Lindsey sleep with her, and she'd tell about the creek with the swimming hole, and the island where great-grandma's ducks and geese slept at night with their heads under their wings to be safe from foxes, and how the lonesome sound of the Hootie Owl up on Sojers Mountain made Ginger, when she was a little girl, burrow down in the feather bed in the dark.

Lindsey plans to go to Sojers Gap someday and see if there's anything left of great-grandma Harkin's house. However, she never mentioned it to Ginger because she didn't want to hear her laugh and say something like, "Why, honey, they's a four-lane highway through that mountain now."

Cassandra Vasik tells the MC she is a hat person. The one she has on looks like something out of Charles Dickens, a stovepipe hat, greenish, like it's been aged in an attic, with a bow in front. Her outfit is composed of just herself and her guitar and one other woman playing board strings.

Cassandra climbs up on her stool and gets ready to sing. When she crosses her knees Lindsey laughs out loud, and M'lindy shoots off the bed and hides behind the drapes. Cassandra Vasik's got on these high-top black lace-up boots like some old toothless grampa rocking on his porch someplace like Sojers Gap.

While Cassandra Vasik sings, Lindsey looks out the window at the rodeo grounds. Cars are streaming into the stubble field they use for a parking lot. If Galen doesn't show up soon, it's going to be plan two. She hates plan two.

She senses eyes upon her, an eerie feeling. But it's just M'lindy, peering down from where she has no business to be, up on top of the valance. She has climbed up the back of the drapes to get there. She will soon have them in shreds. Lindsey picks up a pillow to throw at her and sees the edge up there of what looks like her Game Boy. Super Mario would be a change from books and Sol and TNN.

She gets up and climbs the bookshelves over the bed to reach it, but it turns out to be her Walkman instead.

She turns down Cassandra Vasik and puts on the headset. And here comes Galen's voice. ". . . The very last installment of the Adventures of Omgreeb, King of the Arctic Animals."

She grabs the remote and hits the mute. Now while Cassandra Vasik's cherry red lips move and her face works up expressions fitting to her song, Galen's voice continues, ". . . can't go on much longer. His powers are giving out. The old woman gave them to Omgreeb for as long as victory was his over the forces of evil in the world. But the greenhouse effect is melting the royal ice floe, and oil spills pollute the shores of his consciousness, and seabirds coated with tar die trying to reach the safety of the royal presence, and chemicals in the arctic ice have weakened his powerful flippers and dulled his opalescent scales . . ."

She sits upright in bed. What's Galen up to? When did he make this recording? It's been a couple of years since she last heard an episode in the Adventures of Omgreeb. She's not a little kid anymore.

Jason pounds at the door. "We're on, Lindsey. Come out of there if you're coming to the concert."

She's not.

The final episode. The sound of it gives her the shivers. She will not unlock the door. She will stay where she is and listen to the tape. As soon as she hears the first measure of the first song, she will know if he's back or if they've had to move to plan two.

"If it's plan two," she tells M'lindy, "I'm out of here."

10

Gin ran a tub of hot water and inspected herself in the bathroom mirror. The blood had come from a cut on her forehead. It seemed to be healing, but the knit looked tentative. She cleaned it gingerly with the washcloth, but that started the bleeding again. She pressed a Kleenex to it from a pop-up box supplied by the management, dug a Band-Aid out of her first-aid kit, and pulled the edges together. It felt more numb than painful.

Her forehead would turn blue, then black. A knob was swelling above her eye. Her jaw was squarer than usual. She worked it several times, and except for the squishing sound it made in her ears, it seemed okay.

She felt sleepy, and worried was that a symptom of concussion. She stepped into the steaming bath and sank till she was submerged. She was full of aches and pains.

The Mexican tiles around the tub were creamy, with a few flowered ones scattered around. Restful. Pretty. And the floor was polished Saltillo. A packet of bath oil to dump in the water would be good, but this was no Hilton. She lay there resting on her neck and looked down at her nipples breaking the surface. She'd been run off the road by somebody apparently trying to kill her, she'd seesawed over the black chasm of the Rio

Grande, she'd been rescued by a stranger who materialized out of the night. And yesterday a bear, a bloody corpse, a vanished grave.

At least the grave had been in the scree. So if she'd buried him alive, plenty of air would have gotten through to him in the spaces between the rocks. She closed her eyes and saw again the white of bone breaking through skin. How could anybody in that condition dig himself out? And take the time and trouble, with the bear in the vicinity, to eradicate all signs of blood?

What about that bear? If the victim had been mauled by the bear, where were the claw marks? She hadn't seen any.

A small voice inside her said, the bear was just drawn by the smell of blood.

She slid all the way under and came up and soaped her cropped head. If the victim had managed all these things, why hadn't they seen him on the trail, making his bloody way down the mountain? Immersed again with her eyes closed, as she rinsed she felt again the terror of the dark river and the sickening seesawing of the rig, but she came up smiling, thinking of the woodcutters. She tried to see again the guardian angel. Young, broad, taller than she was. That was all. She lathered all over, stood up and showered off.

The Band-Aid had come off in the water. She was bleeding again. She staunched the blood with another Kleenex, dried herself off, and again dug into her backpack for her minimal first-aid kit—antiseptic cream, Band-Aids in a Ziploc bag, a tube of arnica. She examined the cut. Along her hairline and deeper than she had thought. When she touched it, it gaped. She winced, more at the look of it than anything else. It still felt numb. She applied the cream to the cut and tried pulling it together again with several Band-Aids. She rubbed ar-

nica on her bruises. It was one old folk remedy that
worked.

She was too sleepy to go to the concert. The bed
looked inviting. Warm from the bath, her body clamoring for rest, she fell across the newspaper she was too
tired now to read. She rolled over and pulled it out from
under her and glanced at it as her eyes closed.

They snapped open. She studied the picture. The
headline read: GALEN HAND IN CONCERT TONIGHT.

She had little choice of what to put on. The jeans had
to do, and the flannel shirt. September nights at this altitude were chilly, maybe chilly enough for her light
down jacket. Taos, like Santa Fe, lies at seven thousand
feet, and it's farther north. She needed her sweatshirt,
but she'd buried it on the mountain with the corpse. She
pulled on her thermal top, and over it the flannel shirt,
and dug out her headband to tie around the cut in hopes
of keeping it from opening again.

When she stepped out into the night, she was buffeted
by the music. It was loud, with an insistent beat. She
waited on the shoulder of the highway for a break in the
traffic. Mostly pickups with their truck beds full of music lovers, slowing to turn in at the rodeo grounds.

At the concession stand, Ben Lopez handed over a
sawbuck, took his change, and slipped it in the pocket
of his leather vest. His dinner was a chili dog and a
beer, his third of the evening. He was about to take his
first bite when he saw her. She was crossing the highway on foot, dodging cars. Surprised, he watched her
pass by him in the crowd of pedestrians from the parking field. Bending to his chili dog, he followed.

She climbed the plank steps of the grandstand two at
a time and edged onto the end of a bench. Ben Lopez
stayed below, behind the chain-link fence around the ro-

deo arena. Suddenly everybody was clapping and yelling. Here came the music. But he couldn't clap with his
hands full of beer and chili dog. He finished eating and
slipped the ketchupy paper napkin into his jeans pocket
to keep from littering. He nursed the beer.

He'd come to hear Galen sing. This was the singer's
first performance in Taos, except for those lonely ones
on the mountain. The advertisements had been plastered
around town for weeks. Always before, Galen would
just show up alone in a little Japanese pickup with a
camper shell, and park it at the pueblo while he headed
up the mountain. Nobody'd seen him come down off
the mountain, but he had to be here, he was the star.
Somebody was talking over the mike, but Ben Lopez
wasn't looking at the stage over there across the tanbark
arena. He was looking up into the stands. Her face was
full of bruises. There was a knob on her forehead. And
a trickle of something dark from under her headband.

Gin mopped at her head with her sleeve and bent
her knees aside to let a ten-year-old slither past with
an armful of popcorn in paper bags. Down the row,
squealing siblings reached for the popcorn. This was rodeo grounds all right, redolent of horse manure and hay.
The plank benches were crowded. Somebody the crowd
knew was paged over the speaker system. Everybody
clapped and shouted out the name.

On the makeshift stage a steel player bent and gy-
rated, beating the strings. A pretty bass player with her
flowered dress spread out around her big fiddle smiled
out at the crowd. A drummer—wait a minute, she recognized him. He was the guy in the turned-around baseball hat who'd been eyeing her in the restaurant.
Around her people clapped in time. It was mostly a
young crowd. No headliner yet.

Then the steel player with sideburns grabbed a mike.

". . . Wanna thank y'all for comin' out tonight . . . all this nippy fresh air . . ."

There was an echo in the speakers. Around her people laughed at something she hadn't heard.

"Sorry to be late . . . a little accident earlier in the mountains, folks, but nothing serious . . ." He backed away from the microphone, clapping, and the star leapt onto the stage in a pair of tattered jeans.

Ben Lopez put his fingers to his mouth and shrieked a whistle Galen would recognize. It would tell him Ben was in the audience.

But the singer didn't react. The crowd was too loud. Looked like Galen had barely made it down the mountain in time. He had on old clothes, nothing fancy. Ben moved up to the fence for a better view of the stage.

Gin watched the star come striding to thunderous applause, a glittering guitar slung around his neck. He had on old jeans ripped at the knees and an open jean jacket draped over his shoulders, a white headband, or was it a bandage? and a flowing red silk scarf loosely knotted at his throat. No shirt. Something that looked like a gauzy white sash wrapped around his otherwise bare middle. Before he reached the mike, he was singing, the band coming in behind him.

> If honesty's the way to go how come I'm losing
>   you?
> If spilling the beans is what that means,
>   how come I'm getting my due?

Stomping and singing along, the crowd was wild. She craned around a light post, rising a little in her seat, squinting. For a second she saw two singers, two stages. Some kind of visual distortion due to the lights? She blinked and looked again. Behind her somebody yelled, "Down in front!"

Crouching, she crept down the plank steps and joined the fans crowding the chain-link fence around the rodeo arena. She hooked her fingers in the wire, frowning across the groomed tanbark that put the brightly lit stage at a certain distance from the fans.

The singer swung around, his back to the audience, not singing now, banging away at the guitar, stomping, jerking convulsively with the beat. Like the newspaper picture, he was tall, well built, with long blond hair. He came around again, bending to the mike, cupping an ear to invite the crowd, the crowd responding with the refrain.

He finished the first song, swinging amid thunderous applause into the second. A different pace now, slow and serious,

> Ever'body out there's lying
> Denyin' like me that they're cryin'
> Ever'body out there's dyin'
> Dyin' for love.

The banks of lights on tall metal standards put a glare on the stage. She clamped her eyes shut and opened them again. She shook her head to clear it—it was beginning to throb—but was distracted from the stage by an eerie prickle at the back of her neck. She suddenly felt vulnerable, exposed. Though she couldn't have said how she knew it, she was sure she was being watched.

She swung her jacket over her shoulders and bunched it up around her ears, resisting the urge to turn, and moved behind fans clinging to the wire and swaying in time with the music. She looked for another vantage point from which to see the stage without the glare. As she turned, she caught his eyes upon her. She recognized this one, too, the Indian from the bar. He looked immediately away, but she was sure he'd been watching her.

Up on the stage, the band segued into another number, the audience clapping when they recognized the song, shouting the words with the singer.

> If this is the way you're gonna pout when
> I'm coming in, Get Out!
> If this is the way you're gonna act when
> I turn my back, Relax!

She ducked under a guy wire and stepped up on a block of concrete without a visible function, and squinted again at the stage. Her head began to throb, and her ribs hurt. She felt dazed, more than a little confused. It couldn't be, but the singer up there with long blond hair, prancing around under the glare of lights, was none other than the broken corpse she had buried under a mound of rocks on top of the mountain.

Lindsey has on her baseball cap that Galen brought her from his last tour, an Atlanta Braves baseball cap, navy blue with an *A* on front and a red bill with Deion Sanders' autograph scrawled across it. She prizes that autograph. She was furious when they swapped Deion for Roberto Kelly. That was way back early in the season. But Roberto turned out to be a slugger. The Braves are her favorite team. Galen promised to take her to the World Series. Then just as things were getting really exciting, the baseball strike. Now there won't even be a World Series. She's mad at all of them, players and owners both, though she favors the players.

She's been biting her nails, something she promised Galen she'd quit doing. And she had. They'd been growing out and getting a little shape to them. Cory Lyn promised her a manicure if she kept at it. Not that

Lindsey's into manicures. Now they're wrecked again. She squints at the little black speck underneath one of them. It's not a splinter or she'd have known. Every day it moves closer to the quick. Pretty soon it will emerge like the five-thousand-year-old man from the glacier.

She listens anxiously for the first song. As soon as she hears the opening bars she'll know what's going on. Here it comes, Griff rolling the drums, then Galen's voice over the speaker system. Just as she's feared, it's one of Kylie's mean songs, his old gold record number one. She likes Kylie's mean songs. They're full of pep. But not tonight. Hearing it, she knows what she has to do. Just to be sure, she waits through a couple more songs, but they don't change things. Like it or not, she better get cracking. Grabbing her backpack, she starts stuffing—underwear, sweater, poncho, toothbrush, the last of her candy bars.

M'lindy pounces and lands on the backpack and burrows inside. Lindsey pulls her out. "You'll just have to take care of yourself," she tells her. "No, you will *not* get out of this room. You'll be safe here. Yes, I *know* what I promised. But it can't be helped, this is an emergency."

The only other time she ever left her, M'lindy disappeared. Nobody could find her, she hadn't touched the food or water put out for her. So Lindsey hurried home, and there she was, under the grapevines, her coat a mess and blood in her stool.

As soon as Lindsey showed up, M'lindy cleaned herself, calm as you please, and started eating again. But that eye stayed crossed for days, and she was so mad she wouldn't make up. The vet said she was terrified of being abandoned again. The vet thought somebody had abandoned her in that small-town park that backed up to woods. Or maybe they had stopped like Lindsey for a picnic lunch and left again without knowing their kitten had escaped.

Lindsey hates leaving her again, but it can't be helped. Here comes another of Kylie's old songs. In Galen's arrangement, it sounds like rap.

You don't wanna come and you don't wanna go
You seldom want lovin', it'll mess your pretty bow
Do you want me or don'cha, you better decide
Or what I see comin' is the great divide.

Griff tearing up the drums, crowd going wild, any other time she would love it. Not tonight. Tonight all it does is verify her fears. She holds M'lindy up. "Now listen," she says, up in the little cat face, "don't go to pieces, will you? You'll survive till I get back." But that eye is inching noseward. "Damn it, M'lindy, now don't freak out on me."

But as soon as she lets her go, M'lindy shoots under the covers out of sight.

"Okay, be an idiot."

She grabs the backpack and cracks the door and peers out to make sure the coast is clear. And there's Aunt Glad.

Lindsey cusses under her breath. But Aunt Glad, in her platform pumps, is hurriedly renewing her lipstick in her compact mirror. She snaps her purse shut, puts on her fuzzy pink cardigan, and heads out the door of the bus yelling, "You come lock this door after me, Lindsey, you hear?"

Lindsey watches her cross the worn-out grass to the bleachers and disappear in the crowd. Then she steps out of the bus, shoulders her backpack, settles the Braves cap firmly on her head, and scurries behind the bleachers and across the parking lot, heading for the highway.

* * *

Gin left before intermission, the music blaring behind her and the drums reverberating on the cool mountain air. Her head was bleeding again. She took off the headband and wadded it to the cut, and, plowing free of the crowd at the fence, headed down the dusty entry alongside the stands.

Ahead of her, hurrying toward the highway, was a skinny long-legged kid in baggy green shorts and a yellow Day-Glo windbreaker. On her feet were lime-green sneakers with little lights in the heels that blinked on and off with each step like reconnaissance fireflies zooming low to inspect ant installations. The kid was color coordinated, give or take a little, except for the dark, red-billed baseball cap clamped on by a Walkman headset.

Something about the kid captivated her. Maybe the purposeful way she bent into her walk. Gin wondered if she would ever have a child of her own. The idea of bearing it grandly out in front of her, rearing back for balance to keep from keeling over, was unsettling. But she liked the idea of feeling it inside her, us against the world.

The scout plowed onto the highway under the weight of a forest green backpack stuffed to the gills and zippered tight. It was probably the Walkman that kept her from hearing the noisy pickup bearing down on her, one headlight missing. Gin leapt out and grabbed her by the strap of the backpack and yanked her out of the way. The pickup tires screamed. The child looked up, blinking and straightening her clothes, while the pickup driver pulled away looking shaken.

"Wow, thanks," the kid said. "You, like, saved my life."

One hand still gripping the yellow-clad shoulder, Gin said, "You didn't care for the music?"

"It stinks."

Gin smiled. This was a woman of strong opinions.

"I'm Lindsey." And she stuck out her hand.

As Gin took it, she was struck by the long blond hair, the broad forehead tapering to a chin with an improbably large dimple. What was a kid doing out by herself at this time of night? Gin glanced around, but the two of them were alone there on the shoulder of the road.

"See you," the kid called over her shoulder, waving, the Walkman once more firmly settled over the baseball cap. At a break in the traffic she scooted through.

"Hey!" Gin called. "Wait!" She started across, but a caravan of low-riders cut her off. Craning her neck, she caught glimpses across the highway between the low-slung cars. One minute the child was standing on the other shoulder of the highway. The next, she was walking backward toward town with her thumb out.

"Hey!" Gin shouted again.

A mud-spattered cherry red Jeep pickup paused at the rodeo gate, then leapt into the traffic and swerved past her onto the opposite shoulder. It stopped with the motor running alongside the small hitchhiker. The passenger door opened.

The child in the baseball cap approached warily. The look on her face clearly said she knew better than to do what she was doing.

"Lindsey!" Gin yelled.

But in the passing headlights the piquant face broke into a sudden smile. Of bravado, or recognition? Shrugging out of the backpack, tossing it up, she climbed into the cab of the pickup. A hand reached across to slam the door. Gin watched helplessly as the cherry red pickup pulled back into traffic and bore its small passenger away.

She mopped at the blood on her forehead. She could

cross the highway to her motel and try another Band-Aid, or she could head toward the hospital, farther in toward town. If one Band-Aid hadn't held, why would another? She started walking. A utility van slowed and offered a ride, then pulled away. A pickup passed with whistles and disembodied hands waving out the windows. From a trailing low-rider came hoots and interesting offers. Her destination—she could see it up ahead—lay beyond the traffic light. She had a way to go. She was glad she had on her hiking boots. Not that she'd had much choice.

The emergency room was surprisingly quiet for a Saturday night. Not a soul in sight. She went through the waiting room and entered the unit. A nurse with her back turned stood at a desk annotating a chart. Gin cleared her throat.

The nurse finished what she was jotting down. "You aren't supposed to be in here, hon."

"There's nobody out front."

The nurse glanced with a frown toward the empty lobby. She smiled. "Looks like you've had a little accident."

"Yeah," Gin said. "I'm all right. It's just, this cut keeps bleeding."

"Let's have a look."

Gin allowed herself to be led into one of the curtained cubicles. The nurse patted the examination table. Gin slid onto it and sat there with her hand in her lap and her feet dangling while Nurse Physician Emily Vasquez, according to her name tag, had a look.

"I'm going to take this off," she said, and with a yank removed the Band-Aid. "Have you put antiseptic on this?"

"Yeah, awhile ago."

"It's going to take some stitches."

Gin sucked in her breath. "You think I really need them?"

Nurse Vasquez nodded. "Otherwise, it'll just keep breaking open."

Gin groaned.

The nurse said it wouldn't take long and it wouldn't hurt much. While she cleaned the cut and applied more antiseptic, she asked how it had happened. Gin told her about going off the road in the canyon.

"You were lucky," the nurse said.

Gin smiled. An airplane crash, an auto wreck, or a life-threatening illness, somebody's always there to tell you how lucky you are. "Yeah," she said.

Gin braced herself while the anaesthetic took hold. She didn't feel the needle.

"Thirteen," the nurse said finally, bandaging the cut with gauze. "A Band-Aid would never have held. Let's have a look at the rest of you."

"Must be hard to be on call weekends," Gin said while competent fingers explored her face and neck and probed beneath her hair.

The nurse nodded. "But tonight's been quiet. As you can see."

Gin felt the touch of the cold stethoscope on her back beneath her T-shirt.

"Okay, take a breath."

She did as she was told.

"And now another."

"Were you on call last night, too?"

"Breathe deeply."

Gin breathed deeply.

"Yes," Nurse Vasquez said, "and it was nothing like tonight. We had a bad crash in the canyon. Alcohol related."

"Nobody killed, I hope."

"No, they were lucky."

There it was again. "I've been backpacking in the mountains," Gin said. "I heard somebody had an accident up there." She was fishing.

"Yeah. The singer. Galen Hand. He's performing tonight at the rodeo grounds. You got a hard knock to your chest, didn't you. I'm going to check your blood oxygen." She wrapped a rubber tube around Gin's arm and fastened it. "Okay, hon, make a fist. That's great."

This time Gin felt the needle. She winced. "Were you the one tended to him? The singer?"

"Yep, and he's as gorgeous as his pictures. They've been plastered all over town for a week. We fixed him up. Sprained wrist, small cut on his head and a bruised rib, but nothing serious. Said he'd been digging. Tripped on a root and fell on his shovel. What's your name, hon?"

Gin told her, and she wrote it on the blood sample. "No broken bones, huh?" Gin asked.

"You seem to be okay."

"Not me, the singer."

"Nah, nothing like that." The nurse opened a drawer and brought out a couple of cards with white tablets encased in plastic. "You won't find a drugstore open tonight. Here are some samples. They're painkillers. They may be all you need." She handed Gin a hospital smock. "Here, put this on. And fill out these forms, will you." She handed Gin a clipboard. "I'll get the EKG cart. Then when we're finished here we'll get some X rays."

Oh, crap. "Is all that really necessary?"

"With chest pain it's our policy."

Yes, Gin thought. Self-protection against imaginary lawsuits. It had nothing to do with her cuts and bruises.

If the hospital needed all those unnecessary tests to protect itself, would the hospital pay for them? Dream on.

"I'll be right back," Nurse Physician Vasquez said.

Gin filled out the form on the clipboard while the soft tread retreated down the hall. When the coast was clear, she left the smock on the examination table and snuck out. She got a lift from an elderly Spanish couple just leaving the hospital, a silent ride in an aging Plymouth. The woman held a handkerchief to her lips. She'd obviously been crying. The man commented on the weather and said they needed rain. Gin halfheartedly agreed.

They dropped her at the motel on their way home to Ranchos. Music still blared from the rodeo grounds. Damn, it would be some time before the concert ended and she could try to put all this confusion out of her mind and get some sleep. But the painkiller had begun to work.

She dialed Magda, her sweet, spacey landlady, from the pay phone on the wall outside the motel office. The clerk glanced out at her, then wandered through the door behind the desk that doubtless led to living quarters.

After five rings, just when she was about to hang up, Magda picked up the phone. "Thank goodness you called. We've been worried sick."

"How come?"

"I had a call from the Forest Service. I didn't know what to make of it. We thought maybe you'd been hurt or something."

Right. She'd given Cappabono Magda's number instead of her own. "What did they want?"

"I don't know. He asked if you were back yet. He wanted to talk to you."

"What about?"

"I didn't think to ask."

Magda wouldn't. A picture sprang from her ready projector, of Magda in her Mexican-tiled kitchen with garlic and chili *ristras* hanging from the *vigas*. It made her homesick.

"Did he say what his name was?"

"Yes. Something strange."

"Cappabono?"

"That's it. Is anything wrong?"

Just a bear, a singing corpse, a driver with evil intent running her off the road in the canyon. She said she'd had car trouble and would have to stay over till sometime Monday to get it fixed. Mondays the museum was closed. That was luck. She told Magda where she was staying and gave her the phone number.

Back in her room, she undressed and got in bed. She picked up the *Taos News* and looked at the singer's picture again. She reread the accompanying story. He was on tour, appearances in Denver and Tucson and Albuquerque, and a one-night stand in Taos.

Why Taos? The town was too small for a major star.

The story told of performances since childhood, of his famous parents' deaths in a plane crash, of his recent crowning in Nashville as Country Singer of the Year. The last line in the article read, "The popular young star visits Taos yearly at this time, but this will be his first concert here." She went back over it and read it again. Why would he come to Taos every year?

She studied the picture, three columns wide on the front page. He looked like he was maybe sitting on a stool and bending toward the photographer with an arm resting on his knee, that lionine head of hair swinging to his shoulders, a perhaps unconsciously seductive smile.

She studied the face, remembering the face of the small hitchhiker. The cutline under the picture read:

"Galen Hand, son of Kyle and Ginger Hand of Nashville fame. The poet of country singers carries on the
Nashville tradition."

Grateful for the painkiller, she turned out the light
and lay there, sorting till she fell asleep. Much later she
grew groggily aware of scuffling footsteps approaching
her door. Even drugged by the painkiller, she was suddenly wide awake. Her head was throbbing again. Time
for another pill. She could get addicted to these things.
She rose up on an elbow, listening.

He resented the rush he felt, standing there outside
her door. He badly wanted to see her. And that made
him mad enough to want to turn around and walk away,
wait until morning, have a buddy with him, get her in
the Forest Service office. Anything to make sure he'd
be the one in charge.

He'd stayed clear of women since his wife left him,
taking the boy with her, the boy that couldn't look at
him. Because of the spankings. His wife called them
beatings. Hell, they were nothing like what he'd got
himself from his dear old dad. Now those were beatings.

He loved the kid. Sometimes he loved him so much
there was nothing to do with it but wrestle him to the
floor, teach him to spar with those little fists. He had
hoped she would make him a junior, name him after his
dad, Vic Cappabono, but no.

He'd promised never to lay a hand on the kid again.
What good did that do? He wanted to fall on his knees
and beg, hang onto her hand, tell her how much he
loved and needed her. If worse came to worse, lock her
in and board up the door. Hell, he'd wanted to cry. The
flood would well up in him till he couldn't say anything
to the bitch because if he did he'd whine and grovel. So

all he could do was set his face in a look that said he
didn't give a damn, she could go if she wanted to, he'd
survive. And he had, hadn't he?

And then this tall hiker with her hair cut off walked
toward him down the road. She wore no makeup. She
looked at him out of eyes on a level with his own. She
did nothing at all to acknowledge his maleness, no coy
looks, no helplessness, no leaning on his greater
strength and knowledge of the mountains. And when he
gave her the look, the treatment, she didn't bend.

Later, he'd been disappointed to come upon her camp
and her nowhere in sight. Then when she'd called up to
him he'd wanted to get down off his horse, stay awhile,
shoot the breeze, let her know he wasn't so bad, some-
how undo the way he'd acted the day before. But she
wasn't encouraging, so how could he, without losing
face? You had to keep your dukes up or they'd take
over. Keep 'em in line, let 'em know who's boss.

But this one, he felt like she saw right through him.
She disliked him the minute she laid eyes on him,
didn't want anything to do with him, didn't care to get
to know him. It made him angry, and the anger made
him strong. He'd play with her awhile, cat and mouse,
see if he could scare her a little. It might teach her how
to behave. That would be gratifying.

When knuckles rapped on the door, Gin sat up in bed
and pulled the sheet to her chin. She didn't know a soul
in Taos. Except for Magda and the woodcutters, nobody
knew where she was staying.

"Who is it?"

"It's me, Cappabono. I been in touch with your landlady. She just now told me where I could find you."

She sat there in bed, still groggy, trying to think
about that. "What do you want?"

"I got a few questions."

She pulled on her jeans and T-shirt and went to the door barefoot.

He was a slouched silhouette against lights from the parking lot. Across the way, the music had stopped. She flipped the switch and flinched in the sudden light under the *portál*.

He didn't look at her. He held something up alongside him and bent to look at it. "Can you identify this?"

She stepped out barefoot under the *portál* to make sure he wouldn't step inside. "So," she said, "you found him."

The familiar smirk came back. "Found who?" he asked.

Bastard. She didn't bother answering. "Yes," she said. "I can identify that. It's my sweatshirt. I told you I covered his head with it before I buried him in the scree."

"Oh, yeah, right, the corpse."

What had she ever done to this man? Was it her face, too many bones in it? A jaw too square? Her height? Did she remind him of his mother?

"I got some questions about that," he said.

His truck was parked up by the office. He must have got her room number from the desk clerk. He shuffled his feet like scraping off mud, and almost shyly looked down to watch what his feet were doing. "After I seen you up there, I come on down the other side of the mountain," he said, "toward Red River, inspecting the trails." He looked up at her with those mismatched eyes, the left one pulled down at the corner by the vertical scar. Maybe that's what made him look sinister. Something about the eyes now seemed to plead. He was an odd mix. "On the way down this evening, I met this hiker said his dogs found this a little ways off in the woods."

The sweatshirt hung stiffly. She reached out but withdrew her hand. It had been her favorite sweatshirt, but she didn't want to touch it.

"How come you visited the emergency room out at the hospital tonight?" he asked.

"How did you know I . . . ?"

"We went out there to take this to the lab. Nurse was telling somebody about a patient come in but left before she was finished with her. I was looking over forms filled out yesterday and today, see who might of got hurt on the mountain. And there you were, pretty as you please."

"That's not my blood on the sweatshirt," she said.

"Yeah. I know."

He was waiting for her to ask how he knew. She let him wait.

"But it's human blood all right. And there's too much of it for a superficial wound."

"I told you I used it to try to stop the bleeding. Why is it torn like that?" It was navy blue, heavy and hooded, with a pouch on front.

He looked at it as if seeing its condition for the first time. "Dogs, I guess. Maybe your bear."

Her bear.

"Anyway, we got the hospital lab to check the blood sample the nurse took from you against the blood on the shirt. That's easy enough. And the blood types don't match."

She wondered what her blood type was and why she'd never checked that out. Then she wondered why he'd looked for a match. This was getting eerie.

"So I'm wondering, you want to tell me whose blood this is? You want to tell me what really happened up there on the mountain? Because the dogs had something else they found up there that makes this business take on a whole new complexion."

"What did they find?"

He was looking at her intently, that little smile, watching her reactions. He said it like springing something on her. "They had a body part."

She sucked in her breath and held it, and saw him note that with satisfaction.

"So I come over to ast you not to leave the vicinity. We're going to want to talk to you down't the office Monday morning, soon as the federal marshal gets here."

She was suddenly aware of being very cold. Her bare feet were numb. She stood on one and rubbed the sole of the other down the leg of her jeans. "I've told you all I know about what happened on the mountain. All I can do is repeat it." She hated it that her voice had gone high and thin.

That smirk again. "Yeah. You buried a dead body up there. Some guy a bear had killed. And you don't know who it was. Maybe you could give us a description."

"That's easy," she said. "Wait a minute."

She retrieved the newspaper from the floor by the bed. When she turned, he had stepped into the room. That unnerved her. He flipped on the light.

"Here he is." She handed over the paper. But the man cavorting on the stage tonight had not been missing any of his parts. The innocuous bandages he wore could never have covered the horrific wounds and broken bones of the man on the mountain. It followed that he was not the man on the mountain. She realized she had known it for some time.

She sidled around the ranger to the door. Cappabono looked up from the front-page picture, saw she had moved away, and said with a smirk, "Sure, right. Yesterday he was dead and buried, and tonight he gives a performance for half the population of Taos County."

Across the highway at the rodeo grounds, the banks of lights on their tall standards had gone out, but a highway patrol car with its roof lights on converged with what looked like a sheriff's car coming from the direction of town. Both turned in at the entrance.

Cappabono muttered, "The hell's going on?"

"Something must be wrong over there."

"I'd say you could bet on it. I better go see is he still alive. Maybe he's lapsed back dead." He marched off across the parking lot, his boot heels crunching the gravel.

She went inside for her boots and hopped back toward the door, pulling one on, the other one under her arm.

11

C.C. fumbled for the phone before it stopped ringing, so as not to wake up Miss Eunice. It was after midnight. He was downstairs in his study asleep in front of the television, but the phone also rang upstairs beside their king-size bed. Though he didn't like admitting it even to himself, he'd avoided retiring at the same time as Miss Eunice, but he sorely missed watching her sit at the mirror in her dressing room, smearing her pretty face with cold cream and dropping the Kleenex in her little gilded wastebasket while she stretched her neck, running her fingers down it in search of sag. He wouldn't mind a little companionable sag.

He dragged the phone across the desk toward him by its cord. "Goddamn it," he said into it when he finally got it turned right, "who the devil . . . Hello!"

"Papa? Is that you, Papa?"

"What you think you're doing, calling here this time of night?"

"Papa, you gotta listen, Papa."

C.C. hoped it wasn't a sob he heard on the other end of the line. "Do you know what time it is?" he demanded. "Couldn't this wait till in the morning?"

"Papa, you got to help me."

"Help you! Hell, I told you this was your last chance to be some use to me. Damn it, boy . . ."

"Just give me a minute, Papa. Let me explain."

"What's to explain? Did you take care of it or didn't you?"

"Papa, I did everything I was supposed to do, but everything went wrong and, Papa, you have to help me."

"I don't see how you could louse this up. You're just the delivery boy, damn it. If you can't do this, you won't even work out at Pizza Hut."

"This thing's got me in trouble, Papa. I need you to wire me some money. Now don't, no, don't hang up!"

"Where are you? You back at the ranch? Damn it, Cody, this idn' exactly penny ante."

"No, look, Papa, I'm not at the ranch, I'm still—"

C.C. put his hand over the mouthpiece. Miss Eunice was coming down the stairs in her flowing silk nighty.

"Honey, are you coming to bed?"

"Not right this minute, sugar. Now you go on back upstairs. Don't miss your beauty sleep on account of me."

"Are you on the phone? I thought I heard it ring."

"Yes, sugar. It's just business. Don't worry your pretty head. Go on back upstairs."

"Who is it, C.C.? Is it one of the girls? I hope there's not any trouble." She was standing on the bottom step with a hand on the newel post.

"No. No, the girls are fine. Go on back to bed now."

"Is it Cody? Is it my sweet baby boy?"

C.C. clamped down on the cigar—it hurt his jaw—then took it out of his mouth and with his little finger knocked the ash off on the rug. Such little rebellions satisfied his sense of ownership—of the rug, the house, Miss Eunice.

"Yeah, it's your baby boy," he said, not without sarcasm.

"Oh, let me talk to him!" She was already halfway back up the stairs.

C.C. said into the phone, "What mess've you made for me now? It wasn't much to ast you to do. Now listen, your mother's about to get on the phone and I don't want you to . . ."

"Papa, don't cut me off."

C.C. braced the hand that held the cigar against Miss Eunice's idea of an executive desk—a black slab-marble thing on bowlegs. The hand was shaking. It didn't seem like a part of him. He put the cigar in the ashtray—smoky crystal with a swan's neck curving out of it, he never used the thing—and clamped the offending hand between his thin legs in their paisley pajamas. "Whatever asinine scrape you've got yourself into," he said huskily into the phone, "don't you dare breathe a word of it to your mother, you hear me?"

Then Miss Eunice picked up and he listened in.

"Cody, sweetheart! Are you all right? When are you coming home?"

"Mama, look, I'm fine. Put Papa back on, will you?"

"Boysie, we've got the cutest little blond golf pro at the country club. I've been telling her all about you and she's—"

"Right, Mama, yeah. Let me talk to Papa."

"She's real anxious to meet you. The boys are just flocking after her. They're standing in line for golf lessons."

"Mama, tell Papa he's got to send me some money."

"Her name is Tracy, and she's crazy about cowboys."

"Mama, I'm not a cowboy. You know that. Put me up on a horse, I come off the other side."

Miss Eunice's laughter tinkled like bells. "Aw, honey, you're such a kidder. Now you get on home quick as you can. I can't wait to see you."

"Mama, put Papa back on the line, will you."

"Well, if I do, you've got to promise me my two boys will quit their tussling. Honestly, sometimes I think you two can't get along because you are so much alike."

Downstairs, C.C. was outraged at the insult. He ground the cigar ashes into the dove-gray carpet with the toe of his house slipper and waited for the click when she put down the phone.

"Papa? Are you there, Papa?"

"Where the hell else would I be? Now you listen here to me, Cody. Screw this one up, you're off the payroll."

"Payroll, Christ!"

C.C.'s head leapt back away from the phone.

"Papa, Papa, you never loved me, never even liked me, I know that, but damn it you don't call the twins' allowance *payroll*."

C.C. rolled his eyes up to the ceiling and then had to close them to shut out the plaster cupids flying around up there in baby blue ribbons instead of diapers. Miss Eunice's idea.

"Get aholt of yourself, boy." He clutched his shoulder. He'd been having this muscle pain off and on for some time. He attributed it to not being as young as he once was and Miss Eunice still a lusty woman, which was why he'd altered his bedtime. He dreaded the day when he'd be unable to meet his spousal obligations. Lately his hankering seemed greatly reduced. If his manhood failed him, Miss Eunice would never let on, she was too much of a lady, but he would never be able to hold up his head again.

"Papa you got me into this. It's in your own interest to help me get out."

"What's happened up there? Give it to me straight. Lie to me, Cody, I'll send Ramirez after you." Ramirez was his ranch foreman down in Bandera. "If you didn't

get what I sent you after, you damn well better come
back with the money."

"That's what I'm trying to tell you, Papa."

"If you been to any of them goddamn Indian gambling casinos, I swear I'll—"

"No, Papa. If you'd give me back my credit card, I
wouldn't have to come to you for every little thing.
Papa, I'm twenty years old and not once have you . . ."

"Now you listen here to me. When I was twenty
years old—"

"I know. You came out of the swamp with an alliga-
tor around your neck."

"What? What's that about alligators? Speak up, boy.
Are you talking more of your nonsense?"

"That's how come we never can talk, Papa. What's
sense to me is nonsense to you, and vice versa."

"Don't talk like a fool."

"Fools are the only ones sane, Papa, in a world gone
mad."

This made C.C. so angry he yanked the phone and it
fell off the desk and lay on the rug with a tiny voice
coming out of it. He was shaking all over. He didn't
know how many millions he was worth, but when he
was this good-for-nothing's age he was low man on an
oil rig in Texarkana, covered with the stuff, greasy and
black and stinking, nothing in his stomach but a gnaw-
ing ambition to have as much as that bastard in clean
jeans and Stetson hat who drove out now and then in
his white fishtail Cadillac convertible with the bosomy
blonde snuggled up to the red leather interior, her bare
feet with painted toenails tucked under her and her long
tan arm sliding across the back of the seat toward where
the driver's neck would be if he wasn't standing out
there clear of the rig, the cigar out of his mouth long

enough to peer up with fat-cat satisfaction at the spindly contraption supplying him with liquid gold.

C.C.'s own daddy had been nothing but a pathetic veteran of the CCC, but C.C. had picked up everything he needed in the way of a role model from that hat, that stance, that blonde, and that convertible. He recalled them vividly to this day.

He removed the hand from between his knees but it wouldn't stop trembling. Get hold of yourself, he commanded, but the hand wasn't listening. So with his left hand he picked up the phone and put it on the desk.

"Papa," the tiny voice said, "are you still there, Papa? Papa? Papa? Papa?"

C.C. wasn't sure what happened. When he regained consciousness he was lying on the rug with his face in ashes, clutching his shoulder, and only a dial tone coming at him over the telephone. He would have welcomed a voice, even the boy's. He was scared. He wanted to call Miss Eunice, but he didn't want her to see him like this. He tried to pray, but all he could think was "Now I lay me." That kid's prayer had always scared him, the part about "If I should die before I wake."

He thought he remembered pain. That was before he was on the floor, while he was talking on the phone to Cody, his son and heir.

A spurt of anger increased his circulation and got him up off the floor. He thought he could make it up the winding stairs to bed, and if Miss Eunice was lovey-dovey he could just say not tonight, he had too much on his mind.

12

Lindsey has downed the glass of milk they gave her, more out of politeness then anything else—she's not crazy about milk—while the white dog kept close, rubbing against her leg. It's probably the milk that's made her so sleepy.

The dog's toenails click on the adobe floor. He stands beside the cot, his nose cold on her hand hanging off the bed, a tall, long-legged dog with his ribs showing. She reaches out and pats his head. The cot sags in the middle, wrapping her up and holding her. She can feel the mournful hound eyes on her, keeping her from falling all the way asleep. He licks her hand, so she pats his head some more. They called him Gringo. She smiles, drifting off. They probably call him that because he's white.

The door is open to the outdoors, and Gringo can wander in and out. The room has a fireplace in the corner, and the ceiling beams are logs. She likes the feeling of this place. Nothing fancy about it, no drapes, no padded furniture, no fancy lamps, everything made out of plain wood—table, chairs, the bench against the wall, old-timey kitchen cabinet part-wood part-tin with holes punched in it. A pie chest. Great-grandma had one up at Sojers Gap. Ginger told her. This place reminds her a lot of the old place up Sojers Gap. Of course she's never seen that place. The cabin at Sojers Gap had walls made of logs, but not here. Inside and out, these walls are sand-colored adobe with the straw showing through, flecking them with gold.

Gringo ambles off to flop among the feet under the table in the center of the room lit only by candles. They make a nice soft light but with great big shadows. She's not crazy about the shadows.

"What's that Milli Vanilli she talked about?"

"I don't know."

They're a rock group, Lindsey wants to say. Everybody knows about Milli Vanilli. They're this rock group pulled a lip-sync trick like Byron's. Won a prize doing it, but then it all came out, they didn't get away with it. Byron, he gets away with it. Byron wants to *be* Galen and Galen lets him pretend. Starts concerts with the lip-sync numbers when Galen is late. Signs autographs in Galen's hand when Galen can't stand the crowds, which is more and more often these days. Dresses up in Galen's outfit after a show and pushes his way through adoring fans, signing programs, shirt cuffs, anything they poke at him. Byron comes in handy now that Galen's into his disappearing act. It's how he gets his kicks. That and other ways. She frowns grimly, dozing. Running away from home, even if home is just a tour bus, takes a lot out of you. She's tired to the bone, but what Mary Beth Hale calls "the monkey mind" won't shut up. Across the room they're still talking.

"She says he hasn't come out of the mountain." That's the woman.

"Yes, but I saw him up on the stage, singing and dancing around." This is her guardian angel. When she got in his truck, he already knew who she was, and when she asked how, and what was his name, he said nevermind, just think of him as her guardian angel.

"I was following the backpacker—she left the concert early—when I saw the kid."

I'm not a kid.

"She looks just like him."

"Yeah. There's a strong family resemblance."

"When're you going to get in touch with him?"

"Right now, I guess. I'd better get going."

She feels heavy enough to sink through the floor. It's a real good feeling. She's drifting drifting. She'll soon be gone.

Even this late there was still traffic on South Santa Fe Road. There was no North Santa Fe Road. It was just that the highway south of town was the road to Santa Fe.

Taos was plagued by traffic. For years there'd been talk of a bypass, but it never materialized because businesses opposed it and because its route would not be easy to fix. On one side were the mountains, and on the other mostly *vega* land, good only for pasture because of the high water table. *Vega* land would not support a blacktop. A dirt road across the mesa had lately been paved. Otherwise, traffic was funneled through town.

As they crossed, Gin hopping along, tying her boot laces as she went, surprised, she felt Cappabono's hand at her elbow. The lights of the strip hid all but the dark hard-edge top of the mountain looming to the north. A squad car pulled toward them from the rodeo grounds, drew alongside, and paused at the stop sign. Gin let go of her bootlaces.

Sitting on the edge of the backseat, his hair a mess, was the singer. His eyes registered something like panic. He looked right through her. The squad car swerved onto the highway and sped off.

Cappabono tugged at her arm. They ran across, Gin

looking after the state police car speeding toward town with its roof lights flashing.

"That was him," she said as they hurried past the rodeo arena.

"Who?"

"The singer. Galen Hand. What are they doing with him? Has he been arrested?"

"How would I know?" But he slowed, frowning toward the highway. It was Galen Hand's picture she had showed him. It was Galen Hand he was looking for.

The bus was parked back near a row of cottonwood trees lining an arroyo. The marquee above the wraparound windshield said GALEN HAND. A tan American-made sedan with an insignia was pulled up alongside. The heavy pneumatic door of the bus stood open, spilling a pool of light onto the gravel. Inside, figures surrounded someone seated on a couch—a woman with gold hair and rhinestone eyeglasses. She was sobbing. "It's beyond me. Who on earth could have . . . ? She's been locked in the back room refusing to come out. I never dreamed . . ."

"M'am." The sheriff of Taos County in pale beige trousers and short brown jacket touched her arm gently to get her attention. His black hair held the indentation of his wide-brimmed hat. According to the insignia on the door, the tan car was his. "M'am, if you could just calm down now and answer a few questions, it would be a mighty big help to us in locating the little girl."

The gold head bobbed. Light reflected off the glasses when she looked up. They were pink, the rhinestones at the corners.

"*Bueno*," the sheriff said. "Now, what time was it you last saw her?"

"I don't know. The concert had started. I was hurry-

ing to get over there. You see, my son Byron, he
was . . ."

"That'd be . . ." the sheriff glanced at the man with
sideburns standing beside the couch. Gin recognized the
steel player, slightly built, in dark aviator glasses though
he was indoors and it was night.

"We started around eight o'clock."

A deputy—tan uniform, hat under his arm—stood at
the other end of the couch taking notes. The big drummer stood in the entry to a narrow hallway hugging
himself, and the pretty bass player sat beside the
woman on the couch, holding her hand.

"Okay," the sheriff said gently. "You know she was
here when the concert started. You're sure of that?"

"Well, she didn't say anything when I called back to
her and asked her if she wasn't going to the performance. But she's been in there . . ."

The sheriff swung around to the others. "When was
the last time anybody actually saw her?"

The bass player frowned, touched a lacy handkerchief
to her nose, and shrugged. "She came out around supper time and fixed herself a taco. Then she went back
inside." Nodding toward the back of the bus. "If she'd
come out before the performance, we'd have seen her."

"You didn't see anybody around the bus?" the sheriff
asked the woman on the couch.

"No, but I didn't really look. I was just enjoying listening. My son Byron, you see he . . ."

Gin could have sworn the bass player squeezed the
woman's hand like a warning. The gold-haired woman
pouted. Whatever was about to be said went unfinished.

The sheriff said, "M'am, I see you wear glasses."

They looked about an inch thick, magnifying her eyes
till they took up a lot of her face.

"Yes," the woman said. "I don't have good vision

anymore. There might have been somebody but I didn't see them."

"Do you keep the door here locked when you're in the bus?"

"Usually. If I'm alone or it's just the two of us, Lindsey and me, especially if it's after dark. I make it a habit."

"So it's not probable that someone could just walk in."

"No. I was here in the living area until I went to the concert."

Gin thought she sounded defensive.

"Could the child have opened the door and let someone in?"

She shrugged. "Who would she let in? We don't know anybody here."

The sheriff sighed and hiked his belt, which was weighted down by the .38 revolver. The deputy writing on his pad paused to put his hat on the counter behind him and accidentally knocked something off—a doll with gold pigtails, in a pink dress and a white apron.

"Oh!" the woman exclaimed. "Heidi!" She picked up the doll, hugged it to her breast, and then examined it all over, straightening the dress, retying the hair ribbon. "I think she's all right," she said anxiously. "Is 'oo all right, Heidi?" The doll wasn't saying. She held it up for the sheriff to admire. He stepped back with a painful smile and said, "To get back to the child, now—"

"My son Byron . . ." the woman said. "That's my son Griff," she nodded toward the drummer standing there stiff as a cigar store Indian with his arms clasped over his chest. "Griff is developmentally challenged, but my son Byron, he . . ."

The hand squeeze again, and the pretty bass player

interrupted. "What time was it, Aunt Glad, when you went over to the arena for the concert?"

"Well, it had already started, but just, and I put on my sweater and . . ." The gold head fell. She pressed the doll to her breast and her shoulders heaved with sobs.

"There, Aunt Glad," the pretty bass player said. "Nobody's blaming you. It's not your fault."

"I blame myself, Cory Lyn. She's *gone*." The last was a drawn-out wail.

The sheriff asked patiently, "What makes you think it's a kidnapping? You haven't been contacted? You haven't found a ransom note?"

The gold head shook. "Nooo. Nothing."

"I mean, couldn't she have just taken a notion to . . . ?"

Now the head shook vigorously. "You know what they do. They get aholt of children of the rich, children of celebrities, and ask a fortune for . . . Galen's inherited one fortune and made another. But of course he's had all the advantages while Byron . . ."

Gin saw the hand squeeze again, and again the flow of words stopped. The gold-haired woman looked miffed at being told, ever so subtly, to shut up.

"All right now," the sheriff said, "let's get a clear description. She's skinny and blond, you said, and her backpack's missing. It was green?" He glanced at the deputy with the pad and ballpoint, who nodded he was getting it all down. "*Bueno*. You think she had on a baseball cap. How old is Lindsey?"

Lindsey. Did he say Lindsey? Gin stepped onto the lower step of the bus. "Did you say her name was Lindsey?"

They turned and looked at her.

"Do you know something about this disappearance, miss?" the sheriff asked.

"I think I do."

Cappabono grunted audibly behind her. She heard a lighter click. He'd stayed outside to smoke a cigarette.

"When I was leaving the concert," she said, "I saw walking just ahead of me a child—a girl—in green shorts and a yellow windbreaker and those running shoes with lights in the heels."

The woman called Aunt Glad clutched the pretty bass player, her eyes enormous behind her glasses.

"What time was this?" the sheriff asked, motioning Gin into the bus. She climbed the steps, leaving Cappabono behind. The bus was a sumptuous vehicle—drapes, blinds, overstuffed recliners, a mirrored bar with a forest complete with deer embossed in gold, farther back a dining booth and kitchen. The dark paneling looked like real cherry, not plywood veneer. It was beautiful wood, but it made the space claustrophobic. There was too much of everything. Even the colors were too rich.

"I don't know. It was early," Gin said. "They'd only played a few numbers. I couldn't help noticing her. We were the only ones leaving the rodeo grounds."

"Was she alone?"

Gin nodded. "I didn't see anybody with her."

"All the kids have those shoes nowadays," Aunt Glad said.

"But it was her," Gin said.

She saw the questions in their eyes: Who is this woman? What's she doing here?

The sheriff cleared his throat, ready with the obvious question.

"I know," Gin said, "because she stepped out in front of a pickup. When I pulled her back, we introduced ourselves. She said her name was Lindsey."

They just looked at her.

"It worried me," she said, looking from one of them to another, "a little kid out alone on the highway that time of night." Why was she feeling defensive? "I saw her cross the traffic and start walking backward with her thumb out. She was hitchhiking."

"Oh, my God!" the woman on the couch gasped, hugging the doll.

The pretty bass player asked in an accusing voice that was steely calm, "Why on earth didn't you stop her?"

Gin kept her voice reasonable. "I tried to, but I was blocked by a string of traffic. When I saw her put her thumb out I yelled, but she didn't hear me. She was wearing a Walkman."

The giant drummer nodded. He was good-looking, dark hair and blue eyes, but something strange about him. "Yeah," he said. "She's got her a Walkman."

Gin stared at him. Knotted around his neck was her paisley *panhuello.*

The steel player with the sideburns said, "We *know* she's got a Walkman."

The drummer dropped his head like his feelings were hurt. It was the paisley *panhuello* she was sure she had left by the stream.

"You said she crossed the highway," the sheriff said. "Then she was headed toward town."

Gin nodded. "Before I could get across, a truck pulled over and stopped for her."

The bass player's hand went to her mouth. The nails were long and painted lavender.

"A truck! What kind of truck!" The steel player again. Wiry brown hair a little long and in need of a wash, and then the sideburns.

The sheriff asked, "What's your name, miss?"

Gin told him. He looked over her shoulder at

Cappabono, who had finished the cigarette and stepped into the bus. "What about you, Ranger?"

Cappabono told him. The deputy asked him to spell it.

"Did you get a look at the person or persons in the truck?" the sheriff asked Gin, but he was frowning, looking from her to Cappabono as if wondering what they were doing here.

She said, "There was only the driver. I think it was a man."

"You think?"

"It was the shoulders. They were broad. But . . ." she hesitated.

"Yes?"

"Whoever it was also had long hair, maybe tied back."

"Like a ponytail?" He exchanged a knowing look with his deputy.

The deputy said, "We got a lot of old hippies around here in the mountains."

"Driver was alone?" the sheriff asked.

"One person was all I saw. And he . . . or she . . . leaned over to open the door. I guess if there'd been somebody with him, the passenger would have opened the door."

"Okay, you saw somebody open the door."

She nodded.

"Could you tell what he was wearing—a shirt? Jacket?"

She tried to visualize the hand on the door handle as it swung open. "I think it was a shirt, sleeves turned back at the wrist. A pale shirt—probably white."

"And the child got in the truck."

"Yes. But she looked hesitant, like she knew better."

"Anything said? Any talk between them, could you tell?"

"No. I couldn't tell. But then she smiled at the driver."

"Like she knew him?"

"Maybe. But she might only have been keeping up her nerve."

The deputy asked, "What kind of truck?"

"An old truck. Not ancient, but not new. It was spattered with dried mud."

The sheriff asked, "Did you by any chance notice the license?"

"It was too far away to get the number, but I'm sure it was yellow. Probably New Mexico." Or maybe a dozen other states.

"Did you see what make or model truck?"

"I think it was a Jeep pickup," she said. "Faded red."

The sheriff turned to the deputy. The deputy frowned and shrugged. "They're rarer here than Fords or Chevies."

"Okay," the sheriff said, "let's put out a call." And the deputy picked up his hat and brushed past them out the door.

The sheriff looked past Gin to Cappabono. "Yeah? What is it, Ranger?" Meaning what are you doing here? From the car outside came the crackle and static of the radio, then the deputy's voice.

Cappabono said, "Could I speak to you a minute outside?"

The sheriff looked surprised, but he followed the ranger out the door, leaving Gin standing there with Aunt Glad and the musicians looking at her. Her face felt set in plaster. She tried to smile. When the shriek came from the back of the bus, she realized she'd been hearing something back there for some time, little scratching sounds. Nobody else paid any attention.

"Where has Byron got to? Griff, do you know where Byron is? This'll be the death of me," Aunt Glad said.

The giant drummer hung his head. "You want me to go feed it?" he asked.

It was definitely her paisley *panhuello*.

"I am your mother, and I have asked you a question," Aunt Glad said, but the drummer just stood there looking down at the deep pile carpet.

The shriek came again, followed by a pathetic little cry.

The woman on the couch said, "I knew the minute the child found that cat it'd be nothing but trouble."

The cat set up a steady pitiful yowling.

"Oh, my nerves are driving me *crazy*. I cannot *stand* this. *Will* somebody *please* shut that cat up!" She looked at Gin when she said it.

Gin looked toward the back of the bus. Now the cat's squalling was continuous, either with pain or indignation.

"Well," she said. She liked cats. She still missed Angel, the companion of her youth. Maybe they wanted to get rid of her? "I could try," she said.

The hall passage took her past a kitchen, a bathroom, a room with bunk beds behind folding doors, all the space cleverly used, like maybe on a ship. She'd never been on a ship. Behind her they'd begun talking in low voices.

She cracked the door open at the back of the bus and looked inside. It was a bedroom. Close to the floor a small face peered out.

"No you don't." She bent down and put out a hand. The face instantly disappeared. When she sidled into the bedroom and closed the door behind her, a small part-Siamese, little more than a kitten, leapt from the bed to the heavy drapes and scrambled up to disappear at the top.

The bed took up most of the space, with built-in cabinets and chests. Bookshelves climbed to the ceiling. A door on the right opened to a small bath—toilet, sink, corner shower stall. On the floor, three cat bowls, one filled with dry food, one with water, and the third had recently held . . . tuna, she thought with a sniff.

All she could see up there on top of the drapes were two dark ears tipped forward. Okay, she thought, you can relax up there and size up the situation.

She sat on the bed and picked up the book lying facedown. Nancy Drew. She skimmed a page. In the margin in heavy pencil a child's hand had written, CRAP. She turned back to the title page. "To darling Lindsey on her birthday, from Aunt Glad." The bookshelf in back of the bed held a Sherlock Holmes, a Ryder Haggard, an Edgar Rice Burroughs, and *Riders of the Purple Sage*.

A dartboard hung on the wall at the foot of the bed. The bull's eye was all but obliterated with punctures. Somebody was a marksman.

Gin scratched her fingers lightly on the rumpled sheets—wine and white in a scrolled pattern—and up above, the tipped ears moved forward. Then eyes appeared. She scratched again.

A pale ball of fur landed full force, attacking with sheathed claws. Gin pounced, but she wasn't quick enough. A tail with dark rings disappeared off the foot of the bed.

"You're a fancy cat," Gin said.

No answer. She picked up a lined tablet from the foot of the bed and read,

Dear Mary Beth,

Touring is borrrring. But I've got the cutest cat. I found her in a park where we stopped for a picnic lunch because I was sick of riding riding riding. Her name is M'lindy.

"M'lindy," Gin whispered the name. Me Lindsey. Had the child unconsciously named the foundling after herself?

I've read every book I brought with me. So Aunt Glad went and bought me a new one. Surprise! It's that dumb girl in her sports roadster.

Gin smiled. She liked this kid.

The sheet went taut. A mink-colored paw appeared over the foot of the bed and clung.

With her free hand Gin slid open the drawer of the bedside chest. Aunt Glad's voice came from the front of the bus. "Where can Byron have got to since the concert? I want him here. I need him with me. Griff, I told you to go find your brother."

She heard a moan. From the big drummer? The pretty bass player murmured something. Then the sheriff's voice outside.

The drawer held a deck of cards, a Gameboy, a cellular telephone, an address book, and a scattering of nail files, nail clippers, paper clips, Q-tips, ballpoint pens, a letter that had been opened, and a scratch pad upon which was written, "Lindsey, my girl, behave yourself and don't drive Glad nuts till I get back. Make self at home, but if you leave my room a mess I'll scramble your eggs, you hear me?" The message was followed by Xs and Os. Hugs and kisses.

At the foot of the bed two intensely blue eyes focused on her. Dark tents peaked over them, and white whiskers quivered on a dark, pursy nose. "Come on up here," Gin said. "I won't bite."

In the bookcase over the bed head, between the Ryder

Haggard and *Riders of the Purple Sage*, was a photograph album. She took it down for a look. "The property of Lindsey Hand" was written neatly on the flyleaf, then page after page of family snapshots. Both parents were handsome, the mother pleasantly plump with voluminous red hair, possibly dyed, in the early pictures, but later hollow-cheeked, with outsize blue eyes; the father tall and blond, well built in the early pictures, then farther along in the album, his hair sparse and the beginnings of a paunch.

The kitten M'lindy climbed up on the bed and crouched at the foot, keeping those eyes on her.

As she turned the pages, Lindsey grew from a four-or-five-year-old with a sun squint to a skinny preadolescent, and Galen Hand from a precocious child performer in a cowboy outfit with sheepskin chaps into a handsome young man with strong features and a winning smile.

The family—as individuals and as a group—was photographed indoors and out: in front of a large stone fireplace; sprawled together on a deep white couch with a ceiling-high Christmas tree in the background; in front of an imposing brick mansion with white columns and a circular drive. And Lindsey on a pinto pony, Lindsey in a bathing suit on the end of a pier, Lindsey on Galen's shoulders, both of them in swim trunks with a lake in the background.

Loose in back of the album was a sheaf of publicity shots—of the couple, of each parent individually, of Galen at various ages with his guitar.

M'lindy crept up the bed to crouch beside her. Gin absently scratched her ears. M'lindy closed her eyes and stretched her head up under Gin's hand, but a turned page sent her flying off the bed.

Gin replaced the album and leaned over the edge. No

kitten in sight, only the edge of a magazine half hidden by the bedspread. *Country Music.*

Galen Hand's picture was on the cover. A good smile. White teeth. His hand rested on his guitar, long fingers curled lightly on the strings, and the cover line: IS GALEN GAY? With his fame, sooner or later somebody was bound to come up with that play on his name. And anyway, so what?

She turned to the cover story. WHAT'S GOING DOWN WITH GALEN? the headline wanted to know. Concerts canceled. Fans dismayed. Questions asked. No answers. Was it love? If so, who? Why the mystery? Or grief over the airplane crash? The deaths of Kyle and Ginger Hand a terrible loss to country music. And what about the new album? Terrible songs. No heart. Glum. Grim. With the breath of death in them. Fans angry, drifting. Hints of retirement after the present tour. Could it be illness? Then why so secret? All rumors of AIDS denied.

AIDS. Gin's heart did something incredible. She'd been drenched in his blood. She was full of scratches, her head was laid open. She dropped the magazine facedown on her breast.

It took her a moment to realize the scratches and the cut had come from the accident over the Rio Grande, *after* her adventure on the mountain. Had she had any scratches or cuts on her body before the canyon and the river? Starting at her feet, she reviewed herself, trying to remember. None she could think of. Her heart righted itself.

M'lindy skittered around the foot of the bed, batting a ball of paper across the floor. It came to a rest, and the kitten crouched over it, waiting.

Gin reached down and picked it up and tossed it into the corner. M'lindy leapt after it and came back with it dangling from her mouth.

A retriever. Angel had been a retriever. She'd discovered it when, aged twelve, she'd stayed in bed a week with flu. Angel had brought first a candy wrapper, and then a rubber band. The rubber band had been her favorite retrievable object. No matter how many times Gin threw it, Angel brought it back, leaping up on the bed with it dangling under her determined jaw.

Gin tossed the wadded paper again, and this time M'lindy retrieved it and leapt with it to the bed. It was heavy for her, unweildy. She dropped it on Gin's leg.

The game went on a few minutes more. Then M'lindy tired of it and went to her food bowls. She sniffed the empty. Gin found another can of tuna in the bathroom cabinet. M'lindy watched her empty it in the dish, then crouched over it with her ringed tail wrapped around her. A spoiled cat is a happy cat.

Out front they seemed to have forgotten she was there. She heard voices but couldn't make out what they were saying. She straightened the books and replaced the photograph album, picked up M'lindy's ball of paper from the floor and looked around for a wastebasket. Finding none, she absently smoothed out the paper on the bed. Staring up at her was a photograph much like the publicity shots of Galen Hand lovingly preserved in the back of the album. The difference was, this face was all but obliterated by repeated stabbings with a small, sharp instrument. Puncture holes at the corners suggested the picture had been tacked up and used for target practice. The dartboard.

Had brother and sister had a spat? It seemed likely, siblings being siblings.

She replaced the album, wadded the paper again, and finding no wastebasket, stuck it in her pocket. M'lindy was busy at the tuna. Gin slid into the hallway and pulled the door to behind her.

Up front Aunt Glad still hugged the doll. "Now *where* has Griff got to? *What's happened* to Byron? He was better than ever, wasn't he? The boy is so talented. Galen could do so much for him, if he just would. What on earth could have happened to Lindsey?"

The pretty bass player said, "Maybe she decided to go up the mountain looking for him."

Aunt Glad said, "Lord help us all."

The bass player murmured something comforting, holding the older woman in her arms and patting her back while exchanging a look with the steel player. They barely glanced up as Gin edged past, making for the door.

13

The ringing phone woke him again. C.C. hadn't had many hours' sleep. He didn't move, turn over, let on he was awake. For one thing, he wanted to see how he felt this morning.

"Is that you?" Miss Eunice said with delight. "Hello again, darling."

She never called anybody that but her darling son. He should have left the downstairs phone off the hook when he came up to bed.

Miss Eunice lowered her voice. "Papa's asleep, hon. No, I don't want to wake your father, Cody. He was up late last night. When he came to bed he had a lot on his mind. What is it? Can mumsy do anything?"

C.C. wanted to grab the phone and slam it down in its cradle.

"Well, I don't know, Cody. You know your father doesn't put unlimited funds in my account."

Right. Keep 'em on a short rein. He tightened the muscles in his left arm. They seemed to be in good working order this morning. Can't keep a good man down.

"Well, you know I'll have to ask him," Miss Eunice said, and after a minute, "Well, darling, that's not so easy. You know your father always ... Cody, now watch your language! Yes. Yes, I do know. I realize that, Cody. But you know how it is with fathers and daughters. With you he's only trying to—

"Cody! Now I can't tolerate that kind of talk. Of course I do. You know that. You are my only son."

The voice rose at the other end of the line. C.C. could almost make out the words.

"Now, Cody! Stop it, Cody! No, now, get hold of yourself. You know that's not true. I never ..."

Now the voice at the other end of the line shouted. "... Looking out for yourself! ... just an act! ... put yourself first ... your goddamn bridge game ... country club ... golf ... nothing but a goddamn concubine! Whore!"

Now he'd done it. Under the down comfort, C.C. exulted. *Now* maybe she'd quit trying to slip him money on the sly. *Now* she would see what kind of brat she'd spawned. Serve her right for all the times she'd taken up for him.

A silence had fallen at the other end of the line. Miss Eunice was sobbing. The sobbing got shallower and shallower, and finally turned to hiccups. "How could you say those things to me? I am your mother."

Oh, Christ, now there was sobbing at the *other* end of the line. They were just alike. Except on a son it was unbecoming.

"There, darling. There. Yes, now stop it. It'll be all right. Yes, wait a minute, tell me where to send it." The sound of scribbling on the notepad by her phone, then: "But I don't *understand.* What are you doing *there*? I thought you were out at the ranch. Now, son, that's hardly the case. How can you be anything like a virtual prisoner with thousands of acres to roam around in? You do exaggerate so. Your father's just giving you the opportunity to ...

"Cody! Now stop it, Cody! Don't start that again. That's not true. You know your father . . . You are his only . . .

"Yes. Yes. All right, darling. Yes. All right. Yes, I know you're sorry. Now stop . . . Stop it, Cody! Get hold of yourself. I'll see what I can do."

It won't be a helluva lot, C.C. thought with satisfaction, lying there on his side away from her, feeling stronger by the minute. Last night's spell was just that goddamn wine she was so crazy about, all it was. Stuff didn't agree with him. And he had to cut down some on cigars.

Miss Eunice gently cradled the phone so as not to wake him. He listened to hear if she ripped the address from the pad. She did not. Good. He'd send Ramirez to finish the business up there, bring the cub back from wherever he was, and see he didn't wander off the reservation again.

The moon woke her up, bright as a floodlight shining in her face. Galen once told her the man in the moon watched over her. But Ginger said it wasn't a man, it was a rabbit stirring a bowl of rice. Lindsey can see it both ways, but what would a rabbit want with a bowl of rice? Anyway, now that she's met her guardian angel, who needs the man in the moon?

Everything's very still. She listens hard and hears somebody breathing in the other room. A little while later somebody rolls over and moans or says something in their sleep.

What time is it? Not very late or the moon would be down. Where did she put her railroad watch? It's under the pillow. She drags it out and squints at the luminous dial that gives not only the time of day but the day of the week and locates you in all the time zones across the country. Galen gave it to her, for when they were on the road, so she would know what time it was wherever they were.

Not time yet, unless she wants to stumble around the mountain in the dark. It turns cold at night in these high altitudes. Snuggling deeper under the blankets, she closes her eyes again. But she has to get away before they wake up. She tries to visualize the trail from the Forest Service map Galen showed her, pointing out his route up the mountain. She thinks if she follows the road they brought her down last night, and if it bears northeast, as she thinks it should, she can find the trail. She definitely has a good sense of direction, which is why she sometimes navigates for whoever's driving the bus.

She drifts off again, wakes with a start, then in spite of herself sinks into a deep sleep. Kylie lifts her up in the air, high over his head, and she grabs hold of his hair. It comes off in her hand and she's astonished and frightened. She thinks she has scalped her father. Kylie cusses and sets her down hard, and somebody yells, "It's a rug!"

Now she's on the living room rug at the mansion, playing with somebody's little muppet of a dog. Maybe Reba's. Reba and Ginger are good friends. Reba is saying, "You've got to get rid of him," and Lindsey grabs up the little dog and runs, in case it's the dog they're talking about. She runs through the kitchen where Hattie is cutting the rims off sandwiches.

"Where you going, chile?"

"None of your business!"

She blasts through the back door, crosses the back porch, runs down the path past the trees to the lake, and onto the pier. And there is Byron, smiling at her. "Come here, Lindsey. I'll teach you how to swim."

Back across the grass as fast as she can run. She's never liked Byron, she's not sure why. Where are her shoes? Then somebody grabs her, scoops her up, holds her high. Galen!

She wakes with a start, thinking she's back in Nashville. She lies very still, feeling the sagging springs, aware of the smell of dog. She rolls over and opens her eyes and she's looking down at something white on the floor. The white dog. He rises and stretches and licks her face. Gringo.

She has to get up, find her clothes, locate her backpack. She has to leave before they wake up. The floor is cold with a scatter of sand under her bare feet. There are her L.A. Lights. Great, and her socks stuffed in them. She's still in her shorts. She feels around, finds her baseball cap. She wishes she'd worn her jeans. It's very chilly just before dawn.

She's hungry. There are dishes still on the table. She longs to light the stove and fix a cup of coffee but contents herself with a stale tortilla with something on top of it from somebody's plate. Ug, cold beans. She has tea bags in her backpack. Once in the mountains, she will stop and build a fire and heat some water.

When she creeps out of the yard, the sun's still behind the mountain. She makes her way down an alley between adobe walls. The white dog follows her. She offers him a bite of tortilla, but he sniffs and turns it down and she can't blame him.

Okay, so where is she? She's got to get her bearings. The sun's behind the lower mountain, so that's east. She follows the alley till she comes to a widening, where the paths divide. She takes the one that bears to the north, toward the high mountain. She has her knife with the compass in the hilt, but she doesn't need it yet.

The morning is crisp and the air smells of piñon smoke. She could learn to love the smell of piñon fires. What's that other smell? Barnyards, corrals. It's the rich, country smell of animals. Maybe a little like Sojers Gap.

Farther along, the path becomes a road running along the foot of the mountains. Soon she is in open fields. She can look out and see, far away to the south as the land drops off, the desert with the low purple cones of hills that Galen said were old worn-down volcanoes. When the sun finally clears the mountain, she sees a thread way out there that must be a highway, and the sun glinting off metal. It's a lonely car or truck crawling along it like a metallic ant, though she can't hear it. All she hears are the birds waking up.

Gringo's still tagging along. "Go home," she says. He stops and cocks his head and looks at her.

She walks on, looking back over her shoulder. He's just standing there, watching her. The path has turned into a road that steadily rises. Back where she came from, the whitish fog of wood smoke hangs in a layer over the houses. Above it, mountains rise at the other end of the valley, granite peaks bright in the rising sun. She can see the whole valley nestling in the lap of the mountains. The scene is awesome, not like Mary Beth says it, about any old thing, but really *awesome*.

Bent to the rising road, she hurries now, on the lookout for a trail angling off into the mountain. Gringo pads after her. She picks up a rock and chunks it in his direction.

"Get away! Go home!"

He stops a minute, grinning at her, panting with his

tongue out and hanging to one side like Kylie's tie when he's loosened it and yanked it out of his way.

"Oh, all right. You'll go home when you feel like it. You know your way around here better than I do."

He catches up and they hustle along side by side. Sometimes he runs ahead, then stops and looks back and waits for her like he knows where she's going even if she does not.

"So if you're the scout, show me where to turn off," she tells him.

He trots faster. She jogs to keep up, her backpack bouncing against her back. Then up ahead he stops and waits. When she catches up, panting now, she sees he's at a branching of the trails. He doesn't wait for her but heads up the trail that goes straight for the mountain through the little low evergreens.

"Is this right?"

Gringo runs excitedly ahead of her up the trail.

Ben's side, the north pueblo, won yesterday's foot-race, the feast day was a big success, he and Josie will soon be married and the Beaver finally turned over to the kiva for initiation. But when he and the boy rose this Sunday morning and walked from the hut out by Felipe's pastures to his parents' house for breakfast, they found strange vehicles parked out by the adobe wall and what looked like a conference taking place in the front room.

"What's going on?" the kid asked.

Ben said, "Not your business."

They circled the house, Ben trying to catch what was being said, but the men in there were speaking quietly on the other side of the room. All he heard was ". . . Meeting here today."

Meeting who here?

They found his mother in the kitchen having a second cup of coffee. Breakfast was over, but she'd kept plates warm for them in the oven. She came outside with them and sat under the *sombra* while they ate burritos filled with scrambled eggs and potatoes and onions and chorizo.

Ben looked at her for some clue about what was going on, but she only shrugged and sipped her coffee and looked at the mountain.

"One of the four-bys out front's got a ski valley sticker on the bumper," the kid said.

Ben gave him a look and he tucked his chin into his chest. Ben knew that during the fiesta, in that same front room, Felipe had entertained governors from pueblos to the south, including those from the eight pueblos with gambling casinos. But these could have been strictly social occasions, the governors paying their respects on the saint's name day.

Ben and Hank Sandoz had told Felipe about seeing surveying equipment on the mountain. Felipe had only shrugged. It was not Felipe but the council that called for the watch on the northern border. Then onto the scene came the one they called Buttercup, with the soft thinning hair and the tattoo. Who the hell was he? What he'd tried to do to the long-legged backpacker had Ben worried. That was no accident on the river road.

Too many questions, not enough answers.

All his mother said was, "You want some more coffee?"

Ben nodded and, before she could get up, rose and took his cup inside. No council members in there. Felipe was up to something on his own. He'd often told Ben, "A leader's supposed to lead." When it worked, he was hailed as a great man. When it didn't, it brought the people's displeasure down on his head. Big men always had enemies, Ben told himself, quiet ones with their blankets pulled across their faces, watching and waiting. Also angry young ones, the militants. Felipe ignored them, but Ben feared for his father, what with the watch on the mountain, the ski valley car parked out front, and the governors' visit on the name day. He wanted to know what was going on.

He took his time in the kitchen getting the second cup of coffee. The two groups had separated to opposite ends of the front room, the ski valley pair—an important-looking gray-haired man and the younger one who shot down the cornices—sat quietly at one end, and the Pueblos stood at the other, speaking in low voices. Even if they'd shouted, the Anglos wouldn't have known what they were saying. They spoke in Tiwa.

"So, he has decided."

"He says he has." This was Felipe.

"After all this time?"

"He had a thing to solve."

"And he has solved it?"

"He says that he has."

"Humph. Do you think he is coming?"

"Today, he said."

"At what time today?"

"He did not tell me."

"We are just to wait?"

"Yes, we must wait."

Who were they waiting for? Ben took his coffee back outside and sat on the bench looking at the mountain. He felt a leap of pleasure when Josie rounded the corner of the house. She was in a hurry and out of breath.

"Thank God you're here," she said. "The little sister is missing."

Ben tried to swallow, but the burrito stuck in his throat. He motioned to the kid to run on up the mountain ahead of him. Ben downed some coffee, trying to dislodge the burrito.

"Hurry!" Josie called to the Beaver while she pounded Ben on the back.

14

It had been a late night. Gin felt like she'd just closed her eyes when someone knocked on her door.

Go away. But she wasn't sure she'd said it.

Whoever it was knocked again.

Please go away.

"Are you in there, Ginny Field?"

She opened her eyes. Ginny Field? The guardian angel. "Yes! Just a minute!"

She ran naked into the john, splashed water on her face, decided she looked like roadkill, combed what was left of her hair, and hopping, pulled on her jeans. She was buttoning her shirt as she opened the door.

He leaned toward her smiling, one arm propped on the door frame.

"You called me Ginny."

"Is that not your name? I heard someone call you Ginny last night."

It was not the guardian angel, it was the conquistador.

"Today is my grandfather's ninety-fifth birthday. We're having a celebration out at Soledad's. We thought since you're stranded here without a car you might like to come to the birthday party." His lips inside the soft brown beard were very red. He leaned against the door frame with his hands in his pockets, his eyes smiling, engaging hers.

"There'll be a feed," he said. "Racks of lamb, tubs of guacamole and fresh corn and tomatoes from Soledad's garden . . ."

Today was Sunday. Did she want to stay here alone all day? "I'm convinced," she said. "Let me get dressed."

"But you are dressed."

He was right, what else did she have to put on?

"Maybe you want to comb your hair." He was teasing about her haircut, eyeing her bandage.

"There's not much point."

"There's not much hair."

She glanced over his shoulder toward the rodeo grounds. When she came out of Lindsey Hand's room last night, Cappabono had already left with the sheriff. Nothing for her to do but come back to the motel, but no reason for her to stay there.

"I'll just be a minute."

"That's my truck." He nodded toward a gray extra-cab Toyota pickup parked up by the office. "I'll wait there for you, Ginny."

She ducked under the shower, put on clean underwear, ran a comb pointlessly through her butchered hair, and hurried outside. It was a beautiful day, sky blue and full of sun, and white puffs of cloud over the mountain, the air full of the fresh, resiny smell of piñon.

As they pulled out onto the blacktop, he glanced from her haircut to her feet. His smile scrolled his eyebrows into the bridge of his nose. "Your toes will get cold."

She'd run out with her boots in her hand. "I plan to put these on." But not yet, her feet felt wonderfully free.

They drove past the turn to the plaza. Cottonwoods met over the main street, which was also the highway, and the mountain ahead was a wall of green that looked like it blocked traffic though it was several miles away. Actually, there wasn't much traffic. Everybody who was up had gone to church.

"You've always lived in Taos?"

"I was born here," he said. "All my family is here except for one brother in California. We were here even before it was a Territory."

"I see. Your forebear was a conquistador who stole his land from the Indians." She smiled when she said it.

"That was before my time. And after that you Anglos took it away from us."

"Not I," she said. "I wasn't born."

He laughed. "So," he said, "we have got that out of the way. But you are not one hundred percent Anglo."

"No," she said, and let it go at that. She wouldn't claim her drop of Sioux blood now that being part Indian was 'in.'

About four miles out of town, he slowed at the blinker light and turned right, toward the ski valley. "The Indians want to reclaim this corner and build a gambling casino," he told her.

She frowned. She usually took the Indians' side, but here she wasn't sure.

He took the ski valley highway toward Arroyo Seco. Up on Taos mountain above the timberline, there she was, the Navajo woman weaving. The Navajo woman— a configuration in vegetation against the scooped granite peak—had been weaving up there for centuries. Gin wondered why a *Navajo* woman here in Pueblo country. She thought Navajo weavers had been taught by Hopi women.

"Where are you taking me?" she asked.

"To Arroyo Seco."

"Soledad is your mother?"

"She is my aunt."

"Does she have many children?"

"She has none. She only a few years ago came out of a Carmelite nunnery."

Gin looked at him. He was not kidding. "Aren't they the ones who sleep on straw and can't talk to anybody?"

"She doesn't tell about it."

"She looks very strong."

"I was almost grown before I could beat her at Indian arm wrestling."

"I don't mean strong that way."

He laughed. "Yes. You are right. She is very strong here." He struck his chest with his open hand. "Before she was a nun, when I was a little boy, she taught me to irrigate and garden, she took me fishing, and hunting in the mountains for the winter meat."

They passed through Arroyo Seco and kept going up a dirt road she recognized. He slowed and turned in at the house where she had stopped, hoping to get help, before she ran into Cappabono. It seemed like a long time ago.

It was a sprawling adobe, pickups and cars parked haphazardly in the field in front of it. A pitched roof had been added to what had probably been a flat-roofed hacienda, giving the house an attic with a dormer window where curtains blew in the breeze. The red roof tiles slanted out over a long *portál* with doors opening onto it in the old way. Flowers magenta and purple and yellow grew in hanging baskets under the eaves and, mingling with tomato and pepper plants, made a border around the house. Under the *portál* old men sat in straight chairs, wearing their hats and smoking pipes, talking softly in Spanish. Children ran in the yard. Toddlers wandering in the grass risked being bowled over.

Paco led her around to the back of the house where

the women congregated, setting out food on trestle tables. Slabs of lamb ribs roasted over a pit—she saw smoke rising. Under a big cottonwood beside an acequia, Soledad stirred a pot on top of a cast iron woodstove, and you could hear the sound of running water.

"There you are," a woman called. "Come, my son. Come see your grandpapa."

The old man sat in the shade in an armchair, his hands together in front of him on the head of a white cane. He smiled up with glazed eyes. "Is it you?"

"Yes, Grandfather."

They shook hands but the old man didn't let go. " 'Ave you got a girl with you, Paco?"

"This is Ginny, Grandpa, the one we pulled from the river."

The old man looked in her direction. "You speak Spanish?" he asked.

"Una pocito."

"Bueno. Give me your hand."

She gave him her hand. He nodded. *"Sí.* Is a strong hand."

Paco leaned over and kissed the old man's stubbled cheek. "What can I get you, Grandfather?"

"What kind of Jell-O they got?" Gin saw he was toothless.

While Paco went over to one of the tables, the old man told her, "I see you are good-looking." And laughed at his joke.

She didn't know what to say to that, so she laughed, too. Paco returned bringing a paper plate with orange and red and green Jell-O. The green had marshmallows and chunks of pineapple in it. The old man let go of Gin's hand and took the paper plate.

"Something to drink, Grandpa?"

"Not yet. Beer in a while, not too cold."

She'd seen six-packs in the irrigation ditch, weighted down with rocks to keep them from floating off. Paco went back to the tables. Soledad looked over with a smile. "So," she said, "I am glad Paco persuaded you to come."

"How are you, Soledad?"

"Excelente, excelente."

The ex-Carmelite nun wore a plaid shirt and jeans rolled up over high-top work boots. The other women, all in dresses, looked like they'd come from mass.

"I went to six o'clock," Soledad said, answering her unspoken question. Six o'clock mass, she meant. "I was a nun, you know, but I left the nunnery. The sky in Wisconsin was so gray it made me sick here." She tapped her temple. "I cannot live without the sun." She touched Gin's forehead, tut-tutting over the bandage.

"How did you ever adjust to the world after the nunnery?" Gin asked.

"Hah, I *nayver* adjusted to the nunnery."

They laughed together.

"I thought it would be prayer and hymns and worship of the good Lord. But they had me doing the carpentry." One hand on her hip, she stirred the chili with a long-handled wooden spoon. "My father over there"—she nodded toward the old man—"he made me his boy and taught me everything—stock, crops, carpentry. He could never let me marry, but for the Lord he had to let me go. Now he has me home again."

A woman approached and opened the woodstove's oven.

"This is my sister Petra," Soledad said.

The woman smiled up at Gin with a flushed face, dark hair coming loose in wisps from the heat of the oven. She poked a fork into something inside—Gin smelled cake—and said, "It is too hot to bake inside the house. Out here it is cooler, no?"

Paco came back carrying plastic plates piled high with lamb ribs and posole and guacamole and something smothered in green chili.

"Paco is leaving us soon," Soledad said. "He goes to university to make a lawyer of himself so he can work with water rights. He is the smart one." She laughed. "His brothers, they will stay here and mind the sheep." She reached up and pinched his cheek. "This one is like a son to me."

They sat in the shade on the bank of the irrigation ditch and ate hugely and drank cold beer. Then Paco pitched horseshoes while the women engaged Gin in polite conversation. The cake came out of the oven and Petra presented it to the old man, who ate the first piece with his toothless mouth. Mariaches appeared and people danced under the *portál*. One of the boys brought a pony from the pasture and led the smallest children around in squealing circles on the pony's back. Gin met Archuletas and Armijos and Romeros. Paco was Paco Armijo.

When Soledad finally sat on the curb of the *portál* with a plate on her lap, Gin dropped down beside her. "Paco said you taught him to hunt."

"*Sí*. Whatever he knows, I taught him."

"So you know the mountain well."

"Like the palm of my hand I know these mountains." Soledad laughed. "Every tree up there is a hair of my head."

Gin nodded toward an outcropping with a sheared-off face that loomed beyond the end of the road. "Did you hunt up there?"

Soledad looked up. "We call it the Tooth. Below is a waterfall. *Sí*, I hunted up there."

Paco stood before them, face flushed from sun and horseshoes, wiping the back of his neck with his *panhuello*. By now there must have been fifty people in the house and yard, not counting the children.

Soledad said, "Go away. We are getting acquainted."

"I'm going, I'm going. Can I get you a beer, Ginny?"

"Get iced tea," Soledad said.

As Paco walked off, Gin noticed a new arrival. He wore a Forest Service uniform. How would Cappabono know to look for her *here*?

"Here's Meliton!" the sister Petra said.

Gin was relieved. He was one of the family. Everyone greeted the youth in the Forest Service uniform. The women served him up a plate of food. "But I can't stay," he said importantly. "I am on duty."

They wanted to know why.

"Someone's been killed up there," he said. "A bear, or possibly it's murder."

They clustered around him, questioning.

"Yes," he said, nodding with his mouth full, clearly enjoying the attention. He shrugged. "A suspect, a witness, I don't know. Some Anglo woman. But we don't have the body yet. The search is on the other side of the mountain. I'm driving to Red River." He moved out of earshot, his admirers following.

Soledad looked up from her plate. "So," she said, her penetrating black eyes on Gin's face, "you have been in the mountains. Perhaps you will tell me about it."

Gin thought she had better. And after a halting beginning, she told Soledad of finding the bear and the victim, and of the burial and the vanished body.

Soledad went on eating, not looking at her. "You 'ave had an adventure."

Gin took the Forest Service map out of her back

pocket and spread it over her knees. "It was about here." She put her finger on the map.

Soledad bent over it. "The meadow. Yes, there are berry bushes around the meadow. Perhaps your bear was looking for berries, though they are gone by now. You think the bear has stolen the body?"

"I don't think it was the bear."

Soledad's eyebrows went up. Her dark eyes searched Gin's face. Then, "I believe you. Here," she said, touching the map, "are some old mining claims. Five of them. Twenty acres apiece. One hundred acres surrounded by Indian land and ski valley land. There is an old cabin. About here." The forefinger she put down on the map wore a copper ring. Gin knew what the ring was for. Copper was said to relieve the pain of arthritis. Her grandmother had worn a copper ring. It left a green ring around her finger. For all Gin knew, it worked.

She borrowed a red crayon from some children bent over a coloring book under the *portál* and marked the spot where the cabin was. They pored over the map together. "And just about here," Soledad said, "the stream goes underground as it rounds a cliff, and it comes out"—the ringed finger moved and tapped the map—"here."

"The stream goes through an underground cave?"

Soledad shrugged. "Perhaps. You might call it that. The boys used to dive in holding their breath and come out down below. There are shelves of rock in there. In spring when the snow melts and swells the stream, the rock shelves are covered. Come up for air, there is none. You strike your head underwater on the ceiling. But there will be little water now."

Gin marked the place with the crayon.

"Somewhere around here," Soledad said, "there used to be a hole in the ground. As children we called it the bear hole. Some of the boys showed off by wriggling down into it." She shrugged. "Perhaps it's the entrance to an old mining shaft, or just a prospector's hole. The mountain is pitted with them. Come." She stood up. "We will ask Father."

The old man listened, nodding. "Hah," he said. "Something is hidden on the mountain? What is hidden up there? A treasure? Ha-ha. Yes, there are hiding places. Many times I have been caught by a snow to take shelter with my dog and my rifle."

"And sometimes your daughter," Soledad said.

"Yes, sometimes with my boy." He laughed.

"Where is the bear hole, Papa?" Soledad asked.

The mariaches had stopped playing. They were eating now. You could hear the clink of the horseshoes, the pony's hoofbeats, the squeals of the children.

The old man frowned. "If I could see with these eyes, I could lead you there, but how can I tell you?" He waved them away, or perhaps waved away self-disgust at his infirmity.

"From the meadow, Papa," Soledad persisted. "Tell us from the meadow."

"Hah." Up went his chin. "You must cross the stream. You know the stream? It is on the sunset side of the sheep meadow. There used to be a big tree split in two by lightning. Split right down the middle. You see? And one side laid down and died but the other side lived."

"Yes, Father."

"Straight out . . ." Gesturing with his hand, he searched for words.

"Straight out from the stream? Is that what you are saying, Father?"

"Yes! Yes!" He nodded. "You must pass that split tree and keep it at your back."

Gin was trying to visualize.

"Do you think you can find it?" Soledad asked her.

"Maybe." She nodded.

"Like on a map," Soledad laughed, "it seems clear till you get up there."

"Look out for the bears!" the old man said. "They go soon to their winter beds. Maybe one's in that hole already." He bounced growling at her in his chair, then laughed at his joke.

Soledad took her to the pasture and they chased a paint horse into a fence corner. Soledad grabbed its halter and they led it to the barn where she took down a Navajo saddle blanket and an old Mexican soft leather saddle with a broad low pommel. From the irrigation ditch she took a can of beer and tied it behind the saddle with one of the leather thongs. "For when you get thirsty," she said. "Once, we could drink from the streams, but no longer. Now even those clear mountain streams are polluted."

Gin put her foot in the stirrup and mounted.

Looking up at her, Soledad held onto the stirrup strap. "You sure you want to go up there alone?"

Gin nodded. "I think I have to."

"This horse is called Stump. Behave yourself, Stump."

"Thank Paco," Gin said.

"I will do it. You are not prepared for a night on the mountain. We will look for you back before dark."

Gin crossed the acequia and passed through pastures toward the waterfall. Sounds from the birthday party faded. The paint settled into a little running walk as soon as he hit the road. Higher, against his wishes she slowed him to save his strength, for the trail was climbing.

It had taken her an hour and a half to come back

down, maybe twenty minutes or so to convince Cappabono, if he ever was convinced, and another hour to go back up with the horses. Three hours. Someone had had three hours to unearth the body and hide it, and go back and forth across the meadow carrying blood-stained rocks to pave the floor of the stream. But who? She thought she knew who could easily carry the weight of a hundred-eighty-pound man. Also the stones. How many trips would that take?

She didn't know, but any way she figured it, there was a killer, and the killer was not the bear, and the killer had seen her up there and later tried to send her over the bluff and into the river.

So what are you doing on the mountain, Gin Prettifield?

Looking for the corpse.

Find it, what have you accomplished? Coming up with the corpse might suggest you knew where it was all along. Why not leave it to the rangers? It's their job.

Because I think I know some answers.

She had been sorting, sorting. Her torn and blood-soaked sweatshirt and the "body part" the dogs had found meant the body was still up here somewhere. It followed that the singer cavorting on the stage could not be the broken man she had buried. There had to be two of them. Look-alikes. Witness the photographs on the child's bed, some clearly cherished, one badly defaced.

Movie stars have body doubles. What about famous singers? In the movies they are used in distance shots, where the star isn't needed and a resemblance—size, coloring—is all that's required.

But what about in concert, under lights, with a live audience clamoring at his feet?

Maybe, she thought. On the road, in small towns where the star hasn't performed before. Like Taos.

Then he had to be able to sing as well as the star. How would they find such a double?

It seemed unlikely, but there had to be an explanation. Why go to such trouble?

The magazine articles mentioned disappearances, a possible illness. The musicians had to be in on it, the drummer and steel player, and the pretty bass player. What if Galen Hand were ill, possibly with AIDS . . .

Was that why the body had been made to disappear, to keep the world from knowing? Was that why someone had tried to kill her in the canyon? Because she had seen the body, handled it, buried it? Because possibly the dying man had told her—what?

And then there was the little girl.

You didn't like the music?

It stinks.

She was the singer's little sister. She had to know what was going on, and apparently she hated it. If someone had tried to kill her, Gin, in the canyon because of what she knew, then knowing about the hoax the child could be in danger, too. Was that why she'd run away? Who was the driver of the Jeep pickup? And if the body never turned up, and the sister also was made to vanish, what was to keep the bus from simply moving on to the next concert as if nothing had happened?

15

Lindsey is sitting on a rock taking stock of her situation. She's pretty discouraged. The mountain is different once you're into it, not at all like seeing it in the distance or on a map. The trees are so tall, and there are rocks and cliffs and hills and ravines. And now and then the trails branch and you don't know what to do. She would hate to think she is lost. The sun's straight up and shimmering yellow-green through the leaves. Noon. But her watch tells her it's later. Galen will be pissed.

She'll be okay if she can just find Grampa's old log cabin. Galen keeps it stocked with canned goods. The squirrels and chipmunks eat off the labels—they like the glue—so you don't know what you'll find when you open a can. But it'll be pork and beans, beef stew, spaghetti and meat balls, stuff like that. She's brought along matches. She can have a hot meal if she ever gets there. If she isn't so hungry by then she'll eat right out of the can. She has plenty of water left but she's finished her candy bars.

What's happened to the white dog? He was here a minute ago. Don't panic, she tells herself. You'll feel better if you rest a bit. She doffs the baseball cap and lies down with her head on her rolled-up jacket and turns on the Walkman.

". . . Because Omgreeb's strength is waning, his pearly scales grow dim. Evil forces are closing in. The hole grows ever larger in the ozone layer, there are so many people the animals have no place to live, whole species are dying off, very few Siberian tigers left in the wild . . . oceans of the world polluted, fish full of mercury, high-level waste dumping everywhere, and over a hundred wars waging right this minute over the globe. The earth is sick and dying. And it's the only home we have."

Don't panic, Lindsey tells herself. Stop listening. Up here on the mountain it's hard to believe all the bad things happening to Mother Nature. Birds call to one another up and down the mountain, the aspens bend and whisper. She closes her eyes.

And surfaces later to the smell of burning. The woods are on fire! She sits up, panicked, and sees him sitting there calmly smoking a cigarette. It's only the cigarette that's burning. She skitters backward away from him and is brought up short by the trunk of a pine. Who is he? Some kind of a mountain person? She's read about trolls.

It's Gringo that calms her and takes away her fear. Gringo is sitting right there beside him, getting his ears scratched. Gringo knows this person. So that's where he got off to. He found somebody he knew and left the trail.

"What're you doing here?" At least he talks okay.

"Nothing," she says. "Resting."

"Think you can just take a stroll on Pueblo land and us not know about it? We know ever'thing's going on."

"Yeah?"

"Sure. The birds tell us. The hawks and eagles."

Cool. He talks to the birds. Unless of course he's putting her on. But she heard those birds as she fell asleep.

"You're trespassing," he says. "You'll have to come with me." But he makes no move to leave.

"No, look. I haven't touched a thing on this mountain, honest." Where are you, Galen? Galen will fix it. He's friends with the Indians.

Keep calm, she tells herself. He's just an older kid in a fringed leather shirt and weird-looking shoes. Not even shoes, more like soft leather bags tied around his feet. She would have laughed but she thinks she better be polite. She's on his turf.

"I know who you are. Your name is Lindsey Hand."

How did he know that? "I guess the birds told you," she says with a touch of sarcasm.

He shrugs. "They didn't have to. Stuff like that travels on the wind. You can pick it up if you know how. Your name is Lindsey Hand, and you're kin to the singer."

Something funny going on here. "So okay," she says. "So who're you? What's your name?"

First he says, "Never mind my name." And then he says, "I'm called the Beaver," like he's proud of it.

Okay, she's got something to be proud of too. "Galen Hand is my brother."

"Come along with me, Lindsey Hand." But again he makes no move to get up.

"No, look, I'm hunting for my brother. He came up here and he hasn't come back down. I'll get off your land. I'll get off it as soon as I find those old mining claims. Do you know the way? They're on top of the mountain."

He grinds out the cigarette on a rock, digs a hole with a stick, and buries it. He pats Gringo and Gringo licks his hand. She looks at her watch. She slept longer than she thought. He's looking at the watch, too. She can tell he covets it. Who wouldn't? She's no longer afraid of him. He's just an older kid and a friend of Gringo's. You can trust a dog.

"Tell you what, if you'll take me up there to those old claims I'll give you this." Holding the railroad watch out to him, still on its chain around her neck. She will hate giving it up, but she's got an emergency on her hands.

It doesn't take him a second to decide. He shrugs. "Might as well. Okay, why not? Come on then." Rising, keeping his eyes on her watch.

She stands up and brushes pine needles off the seat of her pants. He reaches for her backpack and hangs it off one shoulder. She's surprised. Is he being nice, or being macho, or about to take off with her backpack? She shrugs. She's been climbing all morning and she's pretty tuckered.

They've climbed maybe half an hour when he puts out his hand and stops her, listening. She hasn't heard a thing. But way up at the top of the aspen belt she sees a movement, somebody up there, moving tree to tree, like hiding. Hiding from who? It's weird. Who else is on this mountain?

He pushes at her with his hand. Get down, he means. Thinks he's in a movie. But she humors him.

"Hey! It's me! Where are you?"

Lindsey snorts a laugh and puts her hand over her mouth. She knows who it is. What's he doing up here?

"Hush up!" her guide says. "Keep down!"

What's the big mystery? It's only Griff.

Cappabono pulled up and sat listening. He thought he'd heard somebody yell. But with wind rising in the aspens, you could imagine anything.

He listened a moment longer, then touched his moccasined heel to the bay horse's side. The rangers were already coming up from Red River. They'd be all over the mountain. His chief thought the body would be over that way because that's where the dogs showed up with the sweatshirt and the other thing.

Cappabono hadn't argued. Let them think what they liked. His chief wanted the mountain searched today, Sunday, because tomorrow morning he'd have to face the federal marshal. Tom Hurleigh, up from Santa Fe, would want to know how come Ranger Cappabono ignored what the woman had told him about burying a body.

He hadn't ignored it, had he? He'd taken her back to the meadow and looked around. No grave. No blood. No body. What else was he to make of it except she was a little nuts, wanting attention? Would the marshal buy that? Cappabono didn't think so, and it made him mad. It was her fault. If she'd treated him different, with a little respect, maybe he'd of . . .

What? a nagging voice asked. What would you have done?

He hated this voice that now and then got after him. It was like a part of him was his enemy, sneering at him, scorning him, putting him down, a part of his own fucking self.

You ought to of looked for the bear, the voice said. It's policy, idn' it? Somebody complains about a bear, you look into it.

He defended himself, his lips moving: I went back up there with her, didn't I? I conducted a search. (That sounded professional.) What more could I of done? I went north on the trail and then south, and I looked.

The voice wasn't buying it: You were going north anyway, south anyway. Glancing around dudn' count.

Maybe a mother with a cub. If she was dangerous, they'd have to shoot her with a tranquilizer and lift her out, and the cub with her, take her way back in the wilderness. If on the other hand she was rabid, they'd have to kill her. He dropped his hand on the rifle butt, then unsnapped the flap on the leather case.

He didn't think the corpse was on the other side of the mountain. He thought the dogs had ranged pretty far. It was Sunday, his day off, but the chief had called everybody in. And Cappabono aimed to find the body, what was left of it. That would be something to hand them. Better late than never.

The voice said: you could of called in for a search, not waited for somebody's dogs to do it, you could of got people on the mountain. You could of brought the backpacker in for a thorough report, find out who she was. Was she some kind of a nut, or a responsible citizen?

They'd checked on her in Santa Fe. Just his luck, she was some kind of art director. What was that, a teacher or something?

What was she doing alone on the mountain? He could have asked her that. She'd say, Just backpacking. What business did she have, a woman, up here on her own? She had something to do with this thing. But what? Said she'd scared off a marauding bear. Who would buy that? Not Vic Cappabono, nosir.

So he'd returned to the motel this morning in his own four-by and parked up the highway on the shoulder of the road, like a stakeout. It wasn't long before this Spanish guy with a beard showed up, knocked on her door, and they went off together. Toward Arroyo Seco and the mountain. Aha.

He followed them at a distance, and they turned in at a house just up the road from where she'd come running down to him with her weird story. He didn't believe in coincidence. He was sure he was onto something. He parked his truck across the road. A party was going on, some kind of a celebration, people eating and laughing and talking. Then music, dancing.

She seemed to be right at home. For a while he lost her in the crowd. Then there she was, sitting there eating on the curb of the *portál*, talking to this gray-haired guy—no, it was a woman—in work boots. That settled it. *She knew these people.* Whatever it was, they were all in on it. Celebrating. Celebrating what?

He'd had to pull farther up the road when the rookie ranger showed up and went right in like he belonged there. Maybe a spy in the ranks of the Forest Service.

You been watching too much television, the voice said scornfully.

He pulled up the bay horse in a clearing and squinted skyward. He'd been lucky. The Forest Service horses had been trucked to the corral at the foot of the mountain in case they were needed in the search. All he'd had to do was whistle and the bay came trotting. He had a saddle in the bed of his pickup.

He'd followed the paint horse into the aspens when he heard the birds. Sometimes the Indians used birdcalls to relay messages, but he knew the difference. These were real birds. Hawks. Crows. Then he saw them wheeling on air shafts way up high.

Buzzards?

He couldn't tell. They were pretty far up. Buzzards, their heads would be bald, reddish, the tips of their wing feathers ragged. Crows, they'd be black-headed, neat and glossy.

The sun blinded him, right in his eyes. He got out his binoculars and tried again. Whatever they were, they were right up there in the sun.

He thought he heard something. She couldn't be far ahead of him. But probably what he heard was the stream. He put his heel to the horse's side and descended to its bank.

Moving forward he heard it again, a rustling in the berry bushes. He stopped and listened, then dismounted, looping the reins around an alder, and crouching crept through alder and scrub oak red now with fall. He came on her suddenly and dropped to one knee.

She was paddling around in the stream, looking for trout. Her cub stood watching on the grass, like wondering what she was doing, then frolicked up and down the bank on the other side and finally waded in, uncertain, then liking it, splashing and playing. Cute little cuss. She went over and boxed his ears for disturbing her fishing, and the cub looked chastened, subdued, making little plaintive whimpers like feeling sorry for himself, and sat on the grass and watched his mama fish.

She was scanning the stream for trout, but then she lifted her head and looked around. She'd got wind of him. She saw him. She stood up on her hind legs and swayed side to side, her black claws folded down on her chest, neat and regular as the teeth on a comb only a lot bigger. She was a great big black mama looking right at him across the stream. He backed away, his heart doing gymnastics, and went to get to his rifle. Let her make one move and . . .

He could bring her down right now. Say she charged him. A bear with a cub, anybody'd believe him. That way, he would have found the killer bear and dealt with her. Would it work?

The backpacker said a cinnamon bear, the voice reminded him.

What's the difference? A woman, he'd say she was nervous, she'd been mistaken, it'd been a black pelt bleached by sun.

The bear stood there watching him. She made an easy

target as she stood there swaying like a tree. He fingered the trigger.

Killing a bear could lose you your job, the voice said scathingly. She's a beauty, too. Look at that pelt. Already thickening up for winter, so pretty it might have been combed.

And look at the cub sitting there with his head dropped off his shoulders, watching the water run. The cub won't survive alone through a winter on the mountain, the voice said.

Cappabono thought of his son, the time he took him fishing in the Pecos. Bears were a lot like people. Certain tribes even called them the bear people.

Stop being silly, he told himself.

Behind him somebody coughed. He started and moved his eye off the rifle sights. It wasn't a real cough, just a fake to let him know they were there. Then he heard them talking that low, choppy Indian talk, making their presence known. Still up here, were they? He had sighted some of them from the ridge the other day, all along their northern boundary. Why? What were they doing there? He knew he wouldn't have spotted them unless they wanted him to.

That one little fake cough was all. But he knew they were over the ridge behind him, though if he turned he would see only aspens, and sunspots moving on the floor of the woods.

He dropped the rifle to his side. The bear growled. He spun around. But she wasn't talking to him, she was telling her cub to vamoose. The cub rocketed up the hillside into the trees, but she stood there on the other side of the stream, her little eyes fixed on him. He backed away, feeling behind him carefully with each foot before he set it down. He was in the alders when she turned and followed her cub up the hillside.

He rammed the rifle into its case and peered over the horse's back into the woods. He knew they were still watching. They hated the rangers. Could they have caused trouble if they'd seen him shoot a bear? Maybe. They knew who he was, all right. Damn Indians.

The big wheeling birds were gone. Where to? If they were buzzards, they'd already found the body. He put his foot in the stirrup and mounted, turning the horse's head up the trail, hoping he hadn't lost the backpacker. He was supposed to be over in Red River. He'd staked a lot on her leading him to the body.

Fuck it. Why hadn't he kept an eye on either the birds or her one, let them lead him to a corpse somewhere up here that was missing a scrap of scalp with long blond hairs attached?

Gin left the paint horse with its reins looped over a juniper branch and crept up the meadow. She heard it again in intervals when the breeze let up. Somebody humming, singing under his breath. So much for solitude. The mountain was populous. Then she saw him. He was up on top of the cliff, reeling along the edge like a tightrope walker over the spot where she'd discovered the bear and the victim.

It was afternoon. The sun had started down the other side of the world, silhouetting him up there with something in his hand, actually something in each hand. As she watched, he sat down hard on the edge of the cliff, then fell aside and caught himself on his elbow. Half sitting, half lying there, he raised something—a pistol!—to his head. Then on second thought lowered it and took a swig from the bottle in his other hand. Christ, he was drunk and contemplating suicide. One thing she didn't need was another corpse up here.

Then he scratched his head with the gun barrel. Not,

she thought, your scratcher of choice. He lifted the bottle to his lips and upended it, looked at it, shook it, and tossed it over the cliff. It shattered with a crash on the rocks below, and he hunched his shoulders and put his arms over his head, like trying to shut out the echoes in the canyon.

It's people like you that start forest fires, she thought with disgust, people like you who poach for trophies on public lands.

But usually such people went farther into the wilderness in their expensive four-wheel-drive vehicles. And they came later in the fall, when they were less likely to be caught up here with their high-powered assault rifles that give the animals nothing remotely resembling a sporting chance. And they came in groups and drank themselves mindless around bonfires that were dangerous at any time of year, but especially in the fall, before the first snows, when the woods are dry.

He got awkwardly to his feet and looked fearfully around, clearly drunk, waving the pistol. She watched him disappear down the other side of the crest. She listened for sounds of drunken laughter or gunshots, expecting his cronies to appear.

She looked at the map to get her bearings. She hadn't bothered to look for the spot where the stream went underground. She figured nobody would find it unless they already knew it was there, and that meant a local, someone who knew the mountain well, had played up here as a child while a father or grandfather drove cattle or sheep to summer pasture on the grassy meadows of public land. And she didn't think the killer was local. Also, that stretch of stream had to be lower down the mountain, where the current gathered volume and momentum, collecting runoff from the mountainsides. She hadn't looked for the cabin. It struck her as being too

far from the meadow. Whoever stole the body didn't
have all the time in the world. He had to use what came
to hand. If the bear cave was where she thought it was,
it was closer, handier.

She'd started across the meadow when here he came,
the drunk from the cliff top, wandering down off the
ridge, skidding in the scree. She would have ignored
him and gone about her business, but he still had the
gun. It hung carelessly in his hand like he'd forgotten it
was there. As he came closer, she was surprised she
recognized him. It was Tattoo from Ogilvie's bar. What
was he doing up here? He'd said he had a plane to
catch.

His other hand held a new bottle by the neck. Did he
have an unlimited stash of booze up here? She'd better
wait till he was gone.

But halfway down the sloping meadow he fell on his
knees and then on all fours and heaved mightily, his
back arching into it, spewing the contents of his stomach into the grass. He kept heaving long after nothing
came up but strings of saliva that hung from his mouth.
And finally, dry retching. He looked down at the mess
he'd made. He dropped lower, wiped the backs of his
forearms on the grass, and blew his nose with his fingers. Gross. Then he crawled over to the stream and fell
flat with his head in the water.

Now, she thought, he'll pass out and drown himself.
But he was scooping water over his head. Then he
pulled back onto the grass and fell facedown.

She waited. He wasn't moving. Good. She got up and
struck out across the meadow.

Lindsey and her Indian guide hid from the drunk in
some bushes with leaves shaped like Christmas holly
and just as scratchy.

"Get down!" Her guide kept tugging at her. "God-damn idiot's got a .45!"

Lindsey didn't know a .45 from a BB gun. She'd lost interest in guns, and her cowboy outfit had long since gone to a Christmas box for the needy. She took it as a sign she was growing up. She wasn't crazy about the idea.

"Quit jerking me around."

"If this was Indian land, I'd . . ."

"What? What would you do?" she asked as scathingly as she could. He was one big show-off.

"I'd take that gun away from him."

"You'd get your head blown off."

"I'm not scared of him!"

Then you've gotta be foolish. "How far's the cabin from here?"

"You climb to the ridge and follow the trail north. After about a quarter mile you'll see it down the other side of the mountain at the edge of a meadow, maybe a couple hundred yards off the rim."

She could probably find it without him. If so, could she keep her railroad watch? But it might be wise to have an Indian guide with you on this mountain, even if he was a show-off teenager.

"Holy Jesus!" he said. She popped up to see what he was looking at, but he yanked her back down by her windbreaker.

"What is it?"

"It's that backpacker girl."

"What . . . ?"

"Shh. Hush. You want them to hear you?"

"We're too far away."

"Sound carries in the mountains."

Like he knows everything. She stuck her head up, and before he pulled her down again she recognized the tall girl who'd grabbed her out of the path of the truck. This was really weird.

She said, "I thought we'd be there by now. We better get going."

"Hold your ponies," Beaver said. Ben was always saying that to him. "I've got to see what the hell's going on. They'll expect a report."

Who, the Indian chiefs? Big deal. She sighed and sat down and stretched out her tired legs and waited. What choice did she have?

16

Gin sat on the grassy margin around a curve in the stream and hidden by a rock pinnacle from the passed-out drunk. She dipped her shirttail in the water and mopped her head and neck. She was discouraged. She'd crossed the stream and searched up and down without finding a tree split by lightning, half of it standing, half lying on the ground. Down below, the paint stretched one foreleg out in front of him, lowered his neck, and reached for a clump of grass. Damn. She knew better than to give him that much slack. He could break the reins. She better go back and shorten them.

But as she started out she heard a voice. She dropped down and anxiously clutched the mossy bank. Then she heard what sounded like a grunt, a little like the snoring-snorting noises of the bear. Her fingers came away clutching something soft and orange-colored beneath the coating of moss. She sniffed. Butterscotch. It was rotting ponderosa wood. She was sitting on a fallen tree so decomposed it looked like the tunnel of some burrowing animal. She looked up. What she'd taken for a rock pinnacle beside her was actually a tall broken-off moss-covered stump.

How long had it been since Soledad's father saw the tree struck by lightning, one half felled, one half still standing? From the look of it, a pretty long time. At

ninety-five, he could have turned over the herding to
sons or grandsons thirty years ago.

Then the voice again, small and close in the immen-
sity of the mountain. She crept toward it and dropped
behind a clump of scrub oak.

"This mountain scary, man. I call, somebody mock
Griff, throw back at him *Hey Hey Hey.* Sound just like
Griff. How they do that?"

A little south of where she would have put the bear
hole, she saw him. He was sitting with his profile to her
and his back against a tree. The big drummer.

"Too many trees. Sick, too, trunks all white. Man,
this mountain something else."

Who was he talking to?

She waited for her heart to slow, then inched closer
and scratched her cheek on the punishing twigs. She
crouched, biting her lip, listening.

"Shut up, Griff."

She scanned the clearing. And there at the other margin she saw who had spoken. He was upended, like
he'd fallen from a considerable height and plowed
headfirst into the ground. His legs twisted and thrashed.
"Get over here, damn it. Help me out of here." His
voice was muffled.

That had to be the bear hole. From what she could
tell, it was fluted at the top, a cornucopia that narrowed
dramatically, holding him caught.

"The wind up here scary, man. Moan like ghosts or
something."

"Shut up with the baby talk."

He was breathing hard, grunting. Gray sweatpants,
sweat-darkened, a few inches of sinewy muscle where
the sweatshirt rode up under him. He was trying to back
out of the hole.

"Damn it, get over here, Griff, you hear me?"

The drummer pretended not to. "I got to go home now. Eat my dinner. Mama she . . ."

"Damn it, quit regressing on me. I need you. Get over here." He backed awkwardly, grunting, the toes in dirty running shoes trying with little success to dig in.

The big drummer clamped his mouth shut and shook his head, though the man in the hole couldn't possibly see. More grunting. Fascinated, she watched the toes of the running shoes try for a little more purchase. She could hear his breathing even when he rested. The muffled voice almost sobbed. "I don't get it."

Her thoughts exactly.

The drummer's mouth drew down at the corners in what looked like a pout.

"Why in the name of . . ."

The drummer looked guiltily down at something he had in his hands. A grass stem he was flattening with his thumbnail. He muttered, "You know."

"Damn it, cut the . . ."

The drummer's mouth tightened like a stubborn child's.

She watched the feet struggle, inching backward. She heard the man in the hole spit something out of his mouth, dirt or maybe twigs. How could he breathe? She didn't think a bear would fit. It was probably, as Soledad said, a prospector's pit partially filled in by the years. Clumps of earth shot up out of the hole behind him like behind a dog after a mole. Then she saw, sitting over in the brush—she couldn't believe what she was looking at—a plain pine box, a coffin.

The drummer said, "Leave it here nobody find it."

Find what?

"Get over here, damn it! Help me!"

The drummer shook his head vigorously, though still the man half buried in the hole couldn't possibly see.

The toes backed. The gray sweatshirt was dark and wet down the spine. The hips swiveled. He wasn't wedged in the hole, he was pulling something out. Gasping aloud with effort, he got his knees under him and, tugging, dragged it faceup out of the pit. It was covered with leaves and twigs and dirt, and it looked very much deader than the last time she saw it. She caught the smell, not quite yet of decay, more like the remembered stench from her childhood, of adobe floors curing. When a neighbor butchered and her grand-mother decided to refinish her floors, they had to leave the house open and stay with neighbors until the stink of the blood subsided, leaving the floors looking like polished Moroccan leather. Nowadays they used linseed oil, not ox blood, as the coagulant.

A wonder the bears hadn't been drawn to the smell. Maybe they had. He'd been stuffed in feet first. On top of the head, a bare spot and something—maybe skull— where the scalp had been torn away. The *body part* the dogs had brought in? Her mouth filled. Oh God, don't let me be sick.

She'd been staring with fascination at the body. Now she looked at the man who'd pulled it out. He was struggling to his knees. Grunting with exertion, he rose, turned, and stumbled into the clearing carrying the body. It was uncanny. They were so alike it was as if he walked toward her holding his own dead and decom-posing self in his arms.

The drummer scrambled up and fell sobbing at the other man's feet, clasping his legs, beating his thighs. "Put it back! Put it back!"

The singer from last night's show freed himself and dropped to his knees and laid the body between them. His face on a level with the drummer's, he said, "Tell me *why*."

As the drummer's face contorted—this was getting surreal—the small hitchhiker in shorts and a baseball cap flew into the clearing.

"What in God's name are you doing here, Lindsey?" the singer cried.

She flew into his arms. "Galen! I didn't think I'd ever find you!"

Then she saw the corpse. Horror burned round dark holes in her face.

"Byron!" she screamed.

Something cold and hard touched Gin above the ear, and a hard, cold hand circled her neck from behind. She gasped and tried to turn, but fingers dug in on either side of her windpipe and a voice whispered in her ear, "Don't move or you're dead."

Then twisting her arm behind her back, he shoved her ahead of him into the clearing. They all turned to look, their faces a frieze of surprise.

"Okay, hold it right there. Don't anybody move."

Lines from a thousand movies, but this was real. Her mouth was dry from the dry mountain air. She closed it. She tried to turn, but the pistol against her temple stopped her. She picked up the pungence of vomit. Tattoo.

"Okay, step back! Get away from him!"

Nobody moved.

"Now!" His shrill voice broke. He waved the pistol. She felt weak with relief that it no longer touched her head, but he was hurting her arm.

The singer reached for the child, but Tattoo grabbed her first, shoving Gin aside.

"Come on," the singer said, "let her go."

"Move! I said move!"

The singer hesitated. Then, "Come on, Griff," he said

softly, taking the drummer's arm. They backed away from the corpse.

"Who are you? What do you want?" the singer asked, eyeing the child Tattoo held close in front of him.

"None of your beeswax."

Gin stifled what might have been hysterics. He was no better at this than at trying to pick her up.

"I know him," the drummer said smugly, proud of himself. "I've seen him before."

Tattoo kept moving the gun from her to the men. "Okay, get down!" he said to her, waving the pistol, pulling the child hard against him.

Gin fell to her knees.

"Now," he said, "don't anybody move or it'll be the last move you ever make."

The drummer's face fell into a look of anger as exaggerated as a mime's. "I saw you before," he said stubbornly. "I saw you up here that day I . . ."

"Shut up!" Tattoo said, putting the pistol to the child's head. "Anybody moves, I'll take her out."

The girl whimpered. He shoved her before him over to the body, then knelt, keeping an eye on them. "Just keep still right where you are."

"Do like he says, Lindsey," the singer said softly.

Tattoo said, "That's right. Mind your daddy."

"He's not my daddy!"

But Tattoo was fumbling at the corpse's silver sand-cast belt buckle. He managed to undo it and snake the belt out through its loops. Eyes on the drummer and the singer, he ran his fingers along it, pressing gently. He smiled. For a minute he seemed to have forgotten them. "Okay, you old bastard," he said, "this here's my payroll." He seemed in a kind of frenzy. Gin realized he was almost as scared as she was, which made him more dangerous.

Tears rolled down the child's smudged face—of anger, it looked like, as much as fear.

Squatting over the corpse, he said, "Okay, little girl, let's go."

He rose and stood there looking uncertain. "Okay, stay where you are or the kid gets it!" He backed toward the woods with the child.

As he backed, with the child in front of him and the pistol at her head, Gin fixed her eyes on the belt looped over his arm. With a silent prayer, she lunged, snatching it and falling over the child. The gun went off. The shot echoed through mountain corridors and ricocheted off the peaks. Was she hit? She felt numb. Looking sideways up, she saw the gun turn on her.

"You asked for it," Tattoo said, bending over, the gun now inches from her head. He pulled the trigger.

Click.

The singer lunged, knocking him down, but the gunman jammed the pistol in the singer's chest and pulled the trigger again. Click. He kept pulling it. Click click. Screaming, crying, "Goddamn it!" Click.

Struggling with the singer, he looked at Gin with hate, as if he knew it was she who'd thwarted him. He wrested the gun from the singer and threw it at her as he went down. Ducking too late, she got it full in the face.

Under any conditions it was brutal, but two blows to the head in two days? Blinded with pain, clutching her head in her hands, she fell. She thought she was dimming out. But she opened her eyes and saw two of everything—trees, people, the coffin. Dizzy at this curious new reality—two of everything—just like the singer, she thought, with his body in his arms.

She seemed to have entered some parallel reality. Was there such a thing?

Then everything faded like a screen gone black, though she could hear all right. Her vision had echoes, but not her hearing. It was all turned around, like the clever jibe from her childhood: your nose is running and your feet are smelling. Ha.

"Are you all right?"

No, I'm not, as any fool could plainly see.

"I don't want to move you." The voice was husky, soft. "You may have a concussion from that blow."

No question about it.

He was holding out his handkerchief. She took it and pressed it to her brow. More blood.

"That was pretty brave, what you did."

"Russian roulette," she said. Her voice sounded all right. "He only had one bullet."

"How could you know that?"

She straightened her leg and waited for the sharp pain shooting through her head to subside. Then she dug in the pocket of her jeans, dredged up five bullets, and held them out like a prize. "The sixth was in the chamber," she said. "I didn't know how to get it out."

She'd stopped long enough as she crossed the meadow to pick up the vomit-spattered .45 in the tail of her shirt and removed these five, but she was stymied by the one in the chamber. She'd meant to save some innocent animal, or a hiker mistaken for a bear, or the drunk from himself. But she'd maybe saved a life. Fancy that.

Lindsey whimpers on Galen's shoulder. She knows she's acting like a little kid but she doesn't care. She clamps her eyes shut against the sight of Byron on the ground. She's overcome by a sick feeling she recognizes. The lady shrink was right. She has this awful power. She *can* will people dead just by being mad at them.

Then Ben Lopez, her guardian angel from last night, comes stalking through the aspens with the Beaver. She eyes her railroad watch hanging around his neck. Maybe she can get it back. He's led her all over the mountain without even coming close to Grampa's cabin.

"She got away from us this morning," Ben Lopez tells Galen. And to her guide, "Run back to the pueblo and tell Josie we found her." The Beaver turns and lopes down the mountain with her watch.

Griff, sitting on the criminal, tells Galen, "I seen him up here before. Not long before you . . ." He clamps his mouth shut and sucks on his lower lip.

"Before I what?"

The man on the ground wiggles, trying to get Griff off him, but Griff just sits there like a rock, shaking his head.

The man groans. Lindsey has never seen him before in her life. Ben Lopez goes over and squats on his heels beside him. Last night Ben picked her up in his truck when she was hitchhiking and took her to his girlfriend's house in the Indian village and fed her cookies and milk. His girlfriend's name is Josie. She's got great hair.

"*I've* seen him before," Ben says, and looks at the girl squatting there on the ground with her head in her hands. "He was at Ogilvie's, in the bar." When she nods, Lindsey sees that haircut. It would have made Ginger throw up her hands. It's the tall girl again, the one who yanked her out of the path of the pickup. And she just now probably saved her life a second time.

Ben says, "Hello, Ginny Field."

"You're the guardian angel."

How does *she* know that?

Ben nods. "I saw this one"—nodding at the criminal—"follow you out of the restaurant. I decided to see what he was up to."

What's going on here? Lindsey's eye glances off Byron, and she thinks of Aunt Glad, who loves him so. She sees the coffin and clutches Galen's shoulder. They're going to put Byron in it and put him in the ground, like they did Ginger and Kylie. Like the lady shrink said, she was mad at them both, and she was mad at Byron, too. So now she's a murderer. She's killed all these people.

Ben tells the tall girl, "He followed you and tried to run you into the river."

"Because I'd seen . . ." She points lamely toward Byron's dead body and says to the man Griff's sitting on, "Then whoever you are, you were up here on the mountain Friday."

Griff mutters, "I saw him."

Lindsey can't make heads or tails of it. All she knows is that Byron is dead and she's glad. Then she feels guilty for feeling glad. Close to Galen's ear, she sobs a little. It works. He holds her tighter.

Then here comes somebody else—a man in a ranger's uniform on a big bay horse and leading another horse, a brown-and-white paint with markings like yin and yang. Cool. She's into horses.

"Found your horse," he says to Ginny Field. From on top of his horse he nods at the body on the ground. "I knew you'd lead me to him." Then he spies the coffin and, Lindsey thinks, his mouth almost fell off. He points to the criminal. "Who the hell's that?"

Nobody answers. They all look at the man on the ground.

The ranger gets slowly down off his horse and takes

his rifle out of its case. He has funny eyes. A scar pulls one of them down at the corner, giving him a bitter look. He's got on moccasins, and he walks soundlessly over to where Griff is sitting. The guy that held her hostage twists his neck and looks up.

"What's your name?" the ranger asks.

The stranger's not saying. The ranger squats over Byron, then looks up at Galen, frowning. "Who the hell're you, his twin?"

"We're cousins," Galen says. "His name is Byron Hand."

The ranger grunts. "Here's where the dogs been at him." Pointing to Byron's head.

Lindsey buries all of her face but the eyes in Galen's shoulder.

"Who's he?" The ranger nods at Griff.

Ginny Field says to Griff, "You're the one moved the body from the meadow and destroyed the grave. And lugged all the bloody rocks across and put them in the stream."

Griff hangs his head.

"What rocks?" asks the ranger.

Ginny Field says, "That's my *panhuello* he's got around his neck. I left it by the stream after I bathed off all the blood."

It's Byron's blood they're talking about. Lindsey can smell it. It's making her sick.

"Finders keepers," Griff mutters, and runs a finger under the bandanna around his neck. Lindsey can't laugh because this is not a laughing matter.

"Why'd you move the body, big fella?" the ranger asks gently, as if he senses something's wrong with Griff.

Griff looks guiltily at Galen.

Galen says, "That's what we'd all like to know."

"*You* know," Griff repeats.

"No. You'll have to tell me."

Griff clamps his mouth so tight his lips turn in.

"Come on, Griff," Galen says softly. "Why'd you kill your brother and hide his body?"

Griff looks up at Galen and his mouth falls open. He bursts into tears—he can cry like a baby—and looks over at the body and starts shaking his head. Shaking it faster and faster, and blubbering, till shaking his head that way, tears streaming down his face, he has to be seeing things in a blur. He crawls over and wipes dirt off Byron's dead face. The criminal starts up, but the ranger shoves him back down again. Kneeling beside the body, Byron combs back the long pale hair with his fingers and says like a little kid, "I put him in a hole in the ground but I din' kill nobody. I wun do that. Griff never hurt *nobody*." And looking angrily up at Galen: "*You* the one, Galen! *You kill Byron!*"

Lindsey grabs Galen around the shoulders and holds on for dear life. Griff doesn't know how to lie. She feels Galen stiffen. Maybe he found out what Byron was up to. But how could he? She never told.

Griff points an accusing finger. "You always say, 'One day I have to kill me a Byron if he don't stop pestering Griff.' "

Yes, Lindsey's heard him say that, but not as if he meant it. But they have to be careful with Griff, because he is literal-minded.

"I know you kill him for me," Griff says. "So I hide him where nobody find him. Not even her." Pointing accusingly at Ginny Field. Why her, Lindsey wonders?

The ranger rolls Byron over on his face and grunts. "I don't know what the hell's going on here, but this man's been shot. This here's a bullet hole, an entry wound."

Lindsey feels light-headed. She might pass out. If somebody shot Byron, does that mean she hasn't killed him by being mad at him?

"No telling if the bullet's still in there. The front of him's too messed up."

Lindsey loses her Milky Ways down Galen's back.

"It's okay, Lindsey-Woolsey." He smooths her hair. "You hid the body to protect me, didn't you, Griff? Because you thought I'd killed him? Is that what you're saying?"

Griff hangs his head. "Sure. I come up here, help you bring Gampa down." He points to the coffin at the edge of the clearing. "We dig him up," he tells them. "He nothing but bones now."

Lindsey feels Galen breathing near her ear. He says softly, "Griff told me he'd hidden Byron's body in a hole. I thought he'd killed him. I didn't know what to do. Since yesterday I've been protecting Griff, and Griff's been protecting me."

The ranger says, "What've we got here?" moving over to the coffin. When he tries the lid, she feels Galen tense up. But the lid's nailed down.

"It's my grandfather's body," Galen tells him.

"Why the devil . . ."

"It's got nothing to do with what happened here."

"Do you own a pistol?"

Lindsey feels Galen shake his head. "I've got an old rifle hidden up at the cabin. It belonged to my grandfather."

With his handkerchief, the ranger picks up the pistol lying on the ground. "Whose is this?"

They all look down at the criminal. He moans and drops his head on the grass. He strikes Lindsey as a sorry excuse for a criminal. He doesn't even look mean.

Galen says, "It's his."

"It's his, all right," says tall Ginny Field.

Lindsey decides to grow some more. Maybe if she eats her vegetables.

The ranger lays the rifle on the ground pointing at the tattooed outlaw, who looks like he's given up. "We'll see if the bullet's still in the body," the ranger says, "and if it came from this gun. What's this?"

The soft leather belt the criminal's clutching in his hand. He doesn't want to let go, but the ranger pries it loose and turns it over. The belt's got a slit at the back, and the slit has a fold.

The ranger grunts. "It's a money belt." He parts the slit with his fingers and dredges something out. Lindsey lifts her head for a better look. It's thousand-dollar bills! The ranger holds them up and they flutter between his fingers.

"Looks like they's lots more where this come from," the ranger says.

The criminal moans, "Daddy Daddy Daddy" just like a little kid, and him a grown man.

17

Gin luxuriates in the clean smell of the rough cotton sheets. She's never slept so deeply in her life. She can't get enough of it. They say it's the concussion. They say they're keeping her at least twenty-four hours for observation, and she's delighted. The food's not great, but they bring it to her, and as long as Soledad's mechanic nephew is still putting the rig back together, she's not going anywhere.

Like answering a question on a test, she tells herself: My name is Gin Prettifield. She's fading again, and the sleep is delicious. They tell her it's healing. It heals the raveled sleeve of . . . ? That's Shakespeare, but what play? Another test of her bruised faculties. She lets it go.

She fades in and out of sleep and is wakened by a low voice speaking. Enough has happened to make her cautious. She lies quietly, listening with her eyes closed.

"Good morning, Ginny. How are you feeling? Are you asleep?" Then he lapses into Spanish, *"Come es que me siento qu le conozeo?"* He's asking in the language of her Mora childhood, how is it that he feels he knows her?

There's more. *"Desde el principio, ie alli, cerca del río vi que estaba distraída y sí batida, pero tambien muy hermosa."* From the first, there by the river, he saw she was distraught and, yes, battered, but also that she was very beautiful.

Soothed by the unexpected warmth, she would like to crawl deeper into the hospital bed, but she doesn't dare move.

Then English again. "I sincerely hope, Ginny, that you will feel better soon. Soledad picked the flowers from her garden and asked me to bring them to you."

But in Spanish, *"Oh Ginny, Ginny, las cogí, cada una, yo mismo, con Soledad se reindo de mi."* (He picked them every one himself with Soledad laughing at him.) *"Ella lee mi alma."* Soledad reads his soul. *"No sabe lo que le digo. Es bueno porque no tengo tiempo para una mujer ahora. Usted sería una distracción, pero mi corazón demande que yo hable, aún en palabras que no comprendiera usted."*

Her face grows hot. Should she open her eyes? She wants to smile. He has told her she will not understand what he is saying, and—*es bueno porque no tengo tiempo para una mujer ahora*—that's good, for he has no time for a woman now, but—*pero mi corazon*—his heart demands that he speak *aún en palabras que no comprendiera usted*, if only in words she will not understand.

"Usted no es cien por ciento gringa, verdad?" (You are not one hundred percent Anglo, are you?) *"Yo puerdo ver por sus ojos."* (He can tell by her eyes.)

Must she lie there and pretend *no comprende*?

Someone enters the room, and to her disappointment he excuses himself and makes a hurried departure.

She wants to call him back. *Vente patras, Paco!* But the newcomer approaches tentatively with something—more flowers, these in that matte green florist paper. Roses. A lot of them, or maybe not. Maybe she's still seeing two of everything.

"Hidy."

She echoes, "Hidy."

"I just thought I'd." He jams the flowers, green paper and all, in her pink plastic water pitcher and sits on the edge of the other bed with his hands dangling between his knees, looking at her with his mismatched eyes out of his poor melting face.

"Things got complicated up there," he tells her.

Maybe he's come to question her, but there are the roses.

He cups his chin in his hand and pulls at it. He twists his head like his collar is tight, but he's got on a striped yellow sports shirt and a charcoal gray windbreaker. He's out of uniform. She'd like to look for the fringed moccasins and the bunions, but she's not willing to lift her head.

"Hurleigh—Tom Hurleigh, he's the marshal—he come up from Santa Fe and we questioned the suspect."

She frowns with the effort to concentrate.

"Killer's name's Chambers. Cody Chambers. He come up here from Texas with a quarter million dollars in thou'd'n dollar bills."

How many thousand dollar bills is that? She feels she ought to know.

Nurse Physician Vasquez sticks her head in the door. "You again!" And laughs, and disappears.

"His daddy's some kind of Texas billionaire. He wanted to get aholt of them old mining claims to look for something called rare earth. Ever hear of it? And this Cody Chambers, he met the dead man, Byron Hand, up on the mountain. 'Course he wasn't dead at the time."

He pauses. She can feel him looking at her to see if she's awake.

"They always used to keep copies of claim papers in

one of the boundary markers. That was supposed to discourage claim jumpers. That's how come they had to meet on the mountain, the impostor and the guy that killed him. The impostor had to get aholt of them papers to work the scam. 'Course they weren't the originals, just copies, but this Chambers guy didn't know that."

She fights off drowsiness. She wants to hear this. But she probably looks like she's falling asleep. He's eyeing her strangely. No, not strangely. It's that eye.

He leans forward with his arms on his knees. Maybe thinking if he gets closer she'll hear better. There's nothing wrong with her ears. Anyway, she knows all this. She and the singer put it together coming down the mountain.

"This Byron, the dead guy that looks just like the singer, he's signed a lot of autographs for Galen Hand because the singer don't like crowds all that much. This Byron guy liked to impersonate him. All the fans, all the women, all that attention. Anyhow, he had the autograph down pat, and he forged the signature on the claim papers."

Was she listening? He couldn't tell. Her eyes kept fluttering, closing, and then she'd open them wide and look right at him. They said she had concussion of the brain. Was that serious? It sounded serious. But they'd let him in. Her face was a mess but looked like it was scabbing over. She had one helluva black eye and a bandage up alongside her temple.

Her good eye opened. She looked at him.

Cappabono nodded and went on. "So I guess they'd just completed their transaction."

Right. And the old young man, this Cody Chambers, had the papers and had started down the other side of the mountain with them, and Byron Hand had the money, which was what he was after, in his money belt, when along came the simple drummer Griff.

She's nodding off, but Cappabono goes on. "So anyway, when this Griff sees his brother he yells at him. Something like, 'Hey, Byron, what're you doing up here? Have you seen Galen?' Something like that."

She smiles at the impersonation and it hurts her cheek. His voice is fading, but the screening goes on inside her head: Cody Chambers hears the drummer call the man he thinks is Galen Hand by another name and comes back up the mountain, full of questions. The drummer goes right on by, heading back to the cabin.

Cappabono's voice stops. She feels him leaning over her to see if she's gone to sleep. She pretends she has.

"Well, anyway," he says, "Byron Hand thinks this Cody guy's caught on that the papers are forged."

That's right, she thinks, and he runs with the money. So Cody Chambers shoots at him, maybe just to stop him. But he hits him, and the guy stumbles and falls over the cliff. Enter the bear.

Cappabono clears his throat. "So okay, this Cody Chambers, he thinks he's killed a man. He's pretty upset. He loses it and runs off down the other side of the mountain. Not to escape, he claims, but just . . . This guy is very . . ." He searches for a word and settles on "excitable."

Gin smiles with her eyes closed.

Gratified, Cappabono chuckles. "I take it that's where the bear come in. Drawn by the scent of blood would be my guess. I doubt the bear ever touched the body. But I guess he wasn't a body yet when you come along."

No. He was alive.

"And like you said," he clears his throat, "you scared the bear off, and Byron Hand died, and you buried him in the scree."

All this was still Friday. What happened to Saturday? Oh, right, she slept on the mountain and woke up Saturday and tried to go on with her backpacking trip. When that didn't work, she came down to Taos.

There are still loose ends she can't tie up. Right now she can't think what. She's drifting. She feels him bending over her and hears him say, very formally, "I surely do hope you'll be feeling a lot better soon." He clears his throat. "Now and then I get down to Santa Fe."

While she takes that in, he stands awkwardly beside the bed. Then he turns and almost runs out of the room. Wow, two in one morning. It must be the haircut.

Later, how much later she doesn't know, the guardian angel arrives. She's clearer now. She's awake.

"Hello, Ginny Field."

"My name," she enunciates carefully, "is Gin Prettifield. Thank you for pulling me out of the rig."

He nods, smiling. His black hair is long and tied in a thong. He has on a plaid flannel shirt and jeans.

"I knew you'd be all right with the Spanish guys," he said.

The woodcutters. The guardian angel was Indian, and the two weren't always friendly.

"I thought you might like to know what was going on up there."

She tells him she knows all about the killing.

"I mean about the old mining claims. The singer has given them to the pueblo. He's been going up there all these years to visit his grandfather's grave and sing him some songs and keep him from being lonely. But now he's dug the old man up and brought him down to take back home and bury him in Tennessee."

She focuses on his face, and there's only one of him. Her head is clearing.

"Felipe—the governor—says we'll lease that hundred acres to the ski valley for a considerable yearly sum. Now that we own the claims, there'll never be any mining up there unless maybe some of our kids would like to pan for gold."

"Good. That's good," she says.

"Anyway, Ginny—Gin Prettifield—you saved some lives on the mountain."

But he can see she's tiring. He leans over the bed and decides she's gone to sleep. He tiptoes out the door and down the hall. He knows now what Felipe was doing with the ski valley people. They were waiting in the front room for Galen. Once he'd figured out what to do about his grandfather, he could sign over the claims to the pueblo, and the pueblo could sign over leases, with carefully worded restrictions, to the ski valley.

All Ben knows about rare earths is that they're the elements of the Periodic Table with atomic numbers 58 through 71, and since the claims were patented early in the century, the village now has both the surface and the mineral rights. They own the land, and Josie is waiting for him out in the parking lot in his old Jeep pickup, and life is good.

"Yeah, but I don't get it."

Lindsey and Galen are sitting together in the horseshoe booth in the bus eating pistachio almond ice cream. Cory Lyn and Jason have gone with Aunt Glad to identify the body, but they can't have it yet because it has to go to the medical examiner's in Albuquerque.

M'lindy, exhausted from anxiety, is sleeping in Lindsey's lap, and Griff is sleeping like a baby back in his mother's bunk, clutching the new doll Savannah that Glad ordered out of a country-music magazine. It has

on a cowboy hat and a print blouse and little suede
boots with fringe on them.

"What don't you get?"

They're eating the ice cream out of a half-gallon car-
ton. She knows the pistachio almond is to distract her
from what all has happened, but she can't get her mind
off it. "Byron looked like he'd been dead too long."

She's built a barrier in her brain against the sight of
Bryon's dead body. She's not telling what Byron's been
up to. Maybe later she will, if it keeps on bugging her.
But if she does, Galen will call in the lady shrink again.

"Too long for what?"

"Too long to of run plan two Saturday night."

"That wasn't Byron, baby, it was me."

She stops with the spoon halfway to her mouth. "I
don't *believe* this. How *come*? I wouldn't of gone looking for you except when I heard Kylie's mean songs I
thought . . ."

"Yeah, I know. You thought it was Byron doing his
lip-sync numbers. Tell you the truth, baby, I didn't give
you a thought. I should have, I know. But I was half
crazy. Griff told me he was glad Byron wouldn't tease
him anymore, that he'd stuffed him in a hole in the
ground where nobody'd ever find him. I thought Griff
had lost it and killed him. Maybe not on purpose, he
doesn't always know his own strength. I couldn't get
him to tell me any more. You know how he is, he'll just
clam up."

Lindsey goes back to the ice cream. She can taste the
green. She finds it consoling.

"I had to buy a little time, figure out what to do.
Aunt Glad would have had a fit if Byron didn't show
up. I couldn't tell her one son had killed the other. You
know how she's always doted on Byron. So I just told

Cory Lyn and Jason I'd changed the opening, and I started out with Byron's lip-sync numbers. That would satisfy Aunt Glad that Byron was onstage. Even sitting in the front row she wouldn't know the difference."

Lindsey says accusingly, "Neither did I."

"I know. I'm sorry, babycakes."

"I was worried sick. I wasn't staying here another night with Byron . . ." She catches herself. She's almost spilled the beans.

But Galen's mind seems to be elsewhere. He nods and she watches him swipe at green ice cream on his chin. With that head of hair, if it weren't for the crew top and clipped sides, he'd look like a cross between Jesus and one of those guys on the cover of one of Aunt Glad's romance novels, naked to the waist and carrying off a heroine with her headlights showing. Except Galen isn't vain, and those guys on Aunt Glad's paperbacks look conceited.

Which reminds her of her Indian guide. She misses her railroad watch. Galen hasn't noticed it's gone. Maybe she can say she lost it. Or maybe she can go out there and get it back. He never got her to the cabin, did he?

"How'd you get so banged up?" she asks.

"Digging up Grampa. I slipped and fell on the shovel."

"I don't know why you had to dig him up."

"I wasn't leaving him up there all by himself."

"You're not going up there anymore?"

"No. Grampa was the reason for the concert in Taos. I had to bring the bus up here so we can carry the coffin home in the hold."

Where the sound boxes travelled. There are things she wants to know, but she has to work up to them. "So what's after Dallas–Ft. Worth?"

"I have to do the national anthem in the Astrodome. That's Houston."

"*I* know it's Houston."

"Right. Sorry, kiddo. Then home for the Country Music Awards."

"Are you going to win again?"

"Nah. They think I've been goofing off."

"Who'll get it? George?"

"I don't know. Maybe Vince."

"I hope it's Vince."

"You like George."

"Yeah, but I love Vince."

"Know something, Lindsey? You're fickle."

"*I* know it."

"Then a video and on to Virginia Beach."

"Can I go?"

"School's starting."

"Can I stay home with Hattie?"

"Home's up for sale."

"But it hasn't sold yet."

"We'll talk about it."

"Galen?"

"Yeah?"

"What're all those weird songs about? How come you won't tell me what's going on with you?"

He frowns and his eyebrows dip like a single wing over his nose.

"I was going to tell you when the time seemed right. But it never did, on account of the tragedy."

She has to think which tragedy.

"We were both still in shock over Ginger and Kylie."

"So who is this John Francis?"

But she's not sure she wants to know. She ducks her head and concentrates on the pistachio. She's read the articles asking why the canceled concerts and where Galen Hand disappears to. She's read the screaming headlines: IS GALEN GAY? She knows about gay. She figures after Byron she knows all there is to know.

"John Francis is a brother."

Is that what gay guys call each other? She's not sure she's ready for this. She tells herself it's okay if Galen is gay. She won't be as jealous of a guy as she'd be of some girl.

"John Francis lives in Kentucky. You know— Kentucky? Where Ginger grew up?"

"He lives at Sojers Gap?"

"Not Soldier's Gap, baby. He lives at a monastery. He's been my teacher. When I went off for a few days now and then, sometimes that's where I went."

Sometimes.

"To a *monastery*?"

He nods, watching her closely.

Wow. This is intense. "What'd you go *there* for?"

M'lindy stretches and resettles with her paw on Lindsey's arm, like holding her down so she can't get away again.

"I went there to pray."

"Pray!" Can he be serious? Yes, he's serious, and he's watching for her reaction.

"Why can't you pray at home? I'll pray with you, if you want to pray." She sounds bitchy but it's either that or bawl.

He's looking at her funny. "I'd made up my mind to become a lay brother."

This is getting scary, so she laughs loudly and repeats, "Lay brother," spewing ice cream all over the Formica. Galen smiles self-consciously, though he doesn't seem to get her meaning. He wipes ice cream off his cheek. Maybe she's hysterical. She grasps at that straw as an excuse for the way she's acting.

Galen says, "I would have to go live at the monastery."

She drops her spoon on purpose. It clatters to the floor. Galen reaches over and takes her hand again. This is too much. She tries to retrieve it but he won't let go. "Don't worry, babe. I saw after the tragedy I couldn't leave you."

"Who said I need you! Who said I need anybody!"

"Well, I need you. You know something, Lindsey. I can't stand a lot more of this surface travel."

A fist grabs her intestines.

"I know, kiddo," he says. "But I'm going to have to fly. I know it makes you feel achy-breaky."

Ouch. She used to say that when she was big into Billy Ray. Now it sounds corny, but she lets it go. "Okay, but only on big planes with the airlines."

He lays his hand on her arm and looks in her eyes. "You know I can't do that, honey. Look, I have to tell you. I've bought another jet." She jerks her hand away but he hurries on. "This plane's got a great safety record and I won't be my own pilot or anything."

"No!"

"No. Now wait, let me . . . Lindsey!"

But she clings to him sobbing. "Don't talk about it!"

"Okay. Okay, baby. I won't, I won't. Eat your ice cream."

The pistachio almond helps her get hold of herself. "What about the postcards?"

"What postcards? Oh, I see. You've been spying on me. Reading my mail." But he's smiling.

"No. It was Ginger. She told me about them, the ones with the bears."

"The bears." He's nodding. "They're from my friend Sam."

Uh-oh. Here it comes. "Sam who?"

"It wouldn't mean anything to you if I told you, and anyway it's unpronounceable. Actually, he's an *angakok*."

"A what?"

Now he's laughing at her. "It's a kind of medicine man. Sam's an Eskimo."

"Like Omgreeb!"

"Yeah. The first time we met, he looked at me for a long time and told me I had an Eskimo inside me. I thought of Omgreeb. I told Sam about him, and he said I'd been Eskimo in a former life and the Adventures of Omgreeb was sort of a memory trace."

"I always knew you were Omgreeb!"

"Come on. I don't believe that stuff. But it *is* strange." His eyebrows go up in twin arcs, black in spite of his hair. "He's a fascinating guy, Sam. Everybody calls him that."

Who is everybody?

"You asked about the postcards. Well, kiddo, they were to tell me where the next ceremony would take place."

What kind of ceremony? "There was nothing on them but some numbers."

"Right. Ten-twenty, say, was October 20th, and the postmark told me where."

"Why the bear?"

"According to Sam, the bear is my totem animal. If the bear was standing up, my spiritual state was OK. On all fours, I was moving forward. Sitting down, I was standing still."

"What kind of ceremony?"

He straightens and puts down his spoon and looks at the table. "Well, you sit around a campfire and you eat ... Well, it's a kind of mushroom."

"Like peyote?"

"What do you know about peyote? I'm taking you out of that boarding school!"

She snorts. "If you think that's a threat, you've got another thing coming. I'd love to come home." Wherever home is. "I've just heard of it is all. Do you have visions?"

"Some do, some don't."

So that's it. Galen's been on a spirit quest. Putting a name to it makes her feel better. She wants to ask about visions, but he's digging into the ice cream again. With Galen, you only get what he wants to give.

He stops eating and plays with the spoon, looking out the window. "See, Lindsey, I've come to feel the human race is doomed and taking the planet to hell and gone with it. We're using up the earth and everything on it— the woods, the air, the seas. And it's too late to do anything but pray."

Fear leaps up in her like she's swallowed a frog.

"See, here's the way the forest works. Leaves catch rain. It trickles down and the soil absorbs it. Some goes into rivers, but most is used by plant roots. A tree can lift water from its roots and up its trunk for over two hundred feet. Then it evaporates and makes clouds, and the clouds hold over two hundred billion gallons that fall down again as rain."

"*I* know all this stuff. I made A in earth science."

"No, but listen. See, it's a cycle, and we're destroying it. We're cutting the forests for lumber. Ranchers burn forest to make pasture, and the pasture is used up in a few years so more forest is burned. No forest, no rain, just drought over the earth, people and animals starving . . ."

She jerks her hand away, but he won't let go.

"No, look, listen to me, Lindsey. We're destroying the ozone layer with stuff like aerosol sprays, and the greenhouse gases that keep the earth warm are increasing. An increase of two degrees will make it hotter than it's been in the last hundred and twenty thousand years. When the ice caps melt, sea levels rise—they think about five feet in the next forty years. That'll flood our Gulf Coast, islands will disappear, New York, Paris, London will all be flooded."

She sees it's got a hold on him. He can't stop.

"There'll be terrible storms, and terrible droughts. No, look, listen to me."

"I have! I've listened! I found the cassette! I heard Omgreeb! It's scary!"

"Sorry, baby. I know you're just a kid. But things are pretty bad with Mother Earth and it may have to be the kids that turn it around."

He's frowning down at their hands. "This terrible pollution makes rain about as acid as lemon juice. It kills whole forests and falls in streams and poisons the fish, and the birds that eat the fish. Forty-eight thousand lakes in Canada alone are threatened, and if that's not enough . . ."

If you can't believe in the earth, what's left to believe in? She yanks her hand free and clamps it over his mouth.

He removes it and kisses the palm. "Okay, baby. I'll quit. But see, Sam told me—and I saw he was right"— Galen's looking right in her eyes—"a song can be a prayer. Maybe if you get a lot of people singing it . . ."

"Everybody sings your songs!"

"That's the ticket, kiddo. I can get a lot of people praying whether they know it or not. It's little enough, but it's what I can do." He puts his arm around her and pulls her close. "See, Lindsey, people think they have to *be* good before they can *act* good. But Sam says it works just as well the other way 'round. Start acting a certain way, like it or not that's the way you'll soon *become*. If we can put something over on people, if we all start singing prayers, maybe we can turn this thing around."

She's nodding her head off.

"I started a song while I was on the mountain." He's got the greatest smile. "I've got the tune, but only a few lines." He steps up on the seat and sits on the back of the booth with his guitar. He always closes his eyes when he sings.

You rock me in your cra-a-a-dle
You feed me from your na-a-ked breast
You bathe me in your warm and gen-n-tle rain . . .
My heart is bare bare bare
And you are rare rare rare . . .
In the universe
Mother Earth . . . something something . . .
Mother Earth.

She closes her eyes the better to hear while he hums on. The tune is lovely, with little Galen-like surprises, and he sings it with the catch in his voice that they all try to copy but nobody else quite gets. It's a love song to Mother Earth. She hopes everybody will sing along.

Rocking back on his heels with his hands in his pockets and a stub of cigar between his teeth, C. C. Chambers peers through the bars at his only son. It gives him a certain satisfaction, seeing Cody in there. Doesn't it prove what he's always known. The boy was born a loser, a throwback to his dear old granddad who stole that 1937 Packard convertible and only by the grace of God and the kindness of some old judge escaped this very fate. Some kind of divine retribution has brought things full circle, for there sits Cody on the edge of his bunk, scrawny, like he's never been fed, with his hair on end and his eyes sunk deep in his head and red from bawling, ending up just like C.C. always knew he would.

"Papa, you can do anything. Get me out of here."

"You've sunk too low this time, boy."

"I never meant to kill anybody. But I had to stop him. I had to come back with the real claim papers or the money one, or you'd of had my hide. I never meant to kill him."

"But after you did, why the hell didn't you run on down there and get the money off him? Nobody'd ever of known you had anything to do with this mess."

"Papa, I'm not as quick as you. I never shot anybody before. Do you know how it feels to think you've killed a man?"

What the hell kind of question was that? C.C. relights his cigar.

"What'd you want with them old claims anyway, Papa? The damn things ruined my life."

"Stop sniveling, boy. Nobody respects a man that snivels. I was after me a pocketful of rare earths. You know what rare earths are, don't you, boy?"

"I don't know much of anything, Papa."

"How'd I get such an ignoramus? Never heard of them, eh? Well, they're a group of chemical elements that's found in soil and rocks. They're so new we don't even know what all they're good for yet. You prob'ly lost me a fortune."

"I'm sorry, Papa. I just felt like the world had come to an end and I'd never ... I didn't mean to kill him, Papa. Maybe I didn't kill him. Maybe it was the fall that killed him. They can tell that from the autopsy, can't they?"

C.C. doesn't know the answer to that, and when C.C. doesn't know the answer he keeps his mouth shut.

"I went back up there to get the money. I got your money back for you, didn't I, Papa? They'll let you have it when all this is over."

C.C. lets him babble on. He's thinking with satisfaction of the effect this will have on Miss Eunice. She's bound to see now that he's always been right about this whelp.

"You got to help me, Papa. Please get me out of here. I can't stand this little cell, Papa. I'll lose it if I have to stay in here, you know that."

C.C. rocks back on his heels, looking down at the big owl eyes looking up at him. The cub has claustrophobia. Serve him right if he goes wild and beats his fists bloody on the walls. C.C. chuckles. "You're on your own, boy. I done all I could for you, and you made a mess of things."

Cody's face contorts. In one spring he's off the bed and up in C.C.'s face. "You goddamn sonofabitch"— shocked, C.C.'s glad the bars are there—"you've never been a father to me. You were out to destroy me from the day I was born. I hate your guts, you hear me? You exploited everybody and everything you ever touched, and I curse every cell in your stinking old body!"

C.C. has fallen back, the pain in his chest so sharp he clamps down on the cigar and bites it in two. The lit half falls to the concrete floor. C.C.'s choking on the other half. He reaches out to Cody for help, but Cody can't get to him. The bars. And Cody is laughing, his only son is laughing while C.C.'s eyes bug and his cheeks engorge and he fights for air. But the rich cigar he's always loved sits like a cork in his craw and blocks out the breath of life.

Lying in the hospital bed looking out the window, Gin tries again to choreograph the dance on the mountain. It's her habit of sorting, getting things straight.

Okay, Galen and his cousin Griff put the pine coffin in the back of the little Japanese pickup, and go up the mountain, taking the Forest Service trail. Byron heads up the trail from the ski valley, and Cody Chambers leaves from Red River to meet him on the claims.

The coffin slowing them down, Griff tells Galen to go on ahead, it's easier for him to heft it to his shoulder and carry it alone. So Galen makes good time getting to the cabin and begins digging up the old grave.

Byron meets Cody and exchanges the phoney claim papers for the money, and Cody starts back down to Red River.

Along comes Griff. Surprised, he greets Byron, calling out his name, and goes on to the cabin.

Cody hears and returns to the ridge full of questions. Thinking Cody's onto the scam, Byron runs, and Cody, convinced he's been had, shoots at him to stop him and hits him in the back. Byron falls over the cliff to the scree below.

Enter a bear, followed shortly by a bucolic backpacker. Cody, atop the cliff, watches as Byron dies in her arms. He panics—he's killed a man—and runs off down the other side of the mountain.

Meanwhile, Griff reaches the cabin and sees Galen all banged up from falling on his shovel. Griff tells him of seeing Byron and another fellow on the mountain. Galen sends him back to find out what's going on.

The bear has ambled off, Byron has died in Gin's arms. Now it's Griff who watches from on top of the cliff as Gin buries the corpse.

Byron is dead, and Galen is injured. Who but Galen has threatened to "kill me a Byron one of these days?" Griff, thinking Galen has done it, watches Gin bury Byron and leave to get help. He digs up the body and hides it, then struggles with the bloody rocks across the meadow and puts them in the stream to wash off the blood. All of this meant to protect Galen: if nobody finds Byron's body, nobody will know Galen has finally carried out his threat.

Griff goes back to the cabin and, meaning to reassure Galen, tells him he "stuck Byron in the ground" where nobody will ever find him.

Galen thinks one brother has killed the other, which means Griff will either go to prison or to an institution. Maybe what's happened was not murder but a fight ending in an accident. He doesn't know what to do.

Cody, fortified by alcohol, gets hold of himself and comes back for the money but finds no corpse.

To buy time, Galen opens the concert with the lip-sync songs to satisfy Aunt Glad. But Lindsey hears them, too, and runs away.

Ben Lopez follows Gin as she leaves the concert because earlier someone—Cody Chambers, because he thinks she's the only one who's seen the corpse—tried to kill her. Ben recognizes Lindsey and gives her a lift to get her off the highway.

When Galen and Griff return to the mountain to retrieve the coffin with the grandfather's body, Griff gives in and leads Galen to the bear hole. Enter Gin, enter

Cody Chambers, enter Cappabono, all looking for the corpse. And enter Lindsey Hand.

It's much too complicated, but she's tried it every which way and this is the only way that works.

Nurse Physician Vasquez sticks her head in the door—"How're they treating you?"—and laughs and disappears.

Then it's Soledad Armijo. Gin is no longer sleepy and she sees only one Soledad. Her head is clearing.

"*E holey!* You don' look good."

Gin smiles.

"The aspens 'ave turned. The mountain is wearing a gold necklace." Soledad smiles at Paco's flowers, touches one of Cappabono's roses. "I see you 'ave many flowers."

"Yes, thanks. Paco was here."

Soledad nods. The black eyes sparkle. She squeezes Gin's hand. Gin feels the copper ring. "I 'ave come to say you are always welcome at my house. I like you. My father likes you. Paco likes you. We all like you. When you come up here, come to us. I will lend you Stump to take you to the mountain. One day I may go with you myself."

"Is that a promise?"

"No." Gin admires the elaborate Latina shrug. "I only say *maybe*. Because if I go up there, I will see my small barefoot self running before me among the trees, and I will *nayver* catch her."

Gin sees the harum-scarum child. Etched in Soledad's face is the map of her life. Which lines, she wonders, are the nunnery?

"I must go." Soledad kisses the big wooden crucifix hanging on a cord around her neck, the figure on it elaborately carved, a little santo, and holds it to Gin's lips. "Get well."

Gin follows her with her eyes out the door, then turns to look out the window at the blue sky and the bluer mountain. It's another gorgeous day in New Mexico.